GREEN

USA TODAY BESTSELLING AUTHOR

T.L. SMITH

WARNING

This book contains sexually explicit scenes and adult language and may be considered offensive to some readers. This book is intended for adults ONLY. Please store your files wisely, where they cannot be accessed by under-aged readers.

Cover – RBA

Edited – Swish Editing

Proofread – Contagious Edits

BLURB

Things have changed, some things stay the same.

One thing I know for sure, no matter what, Rose will forever be mine.

In this life and the next.

Even if I break her wish, even if I break her heart.

Some things are hard to let go.

Harder than I anticipated.

And that's okay.

I'll have to keep it hidden, even on her favorite holiday of the year.

I will keep this secret.

Merry 'Black' Christmas.

1

BLACK

I t happens when it is at its darkest, when the night's sky is black, when the cold wind hits you hard. Pinches at you and uses you as its weapon.

That's when it happens.

That's when I do the unthinkable.

Something I never thought I'd do again.

But the darkness, the blackness takes hold of me, as it has on more than one occasion. And when it calls. It's almost impossible to say no.

The crunch under my boots brings back memories, memories of times when I never had to think about anyone but myself. Honestly, at that time I couldn't have cared less about anyone.

But now I have more.

Way more than I ever intended to have in my life.

My life is almost picture perfect.

My family's complete.

My life, to some, is almost perfect.

She makes it that way just by being herself.

My Rose.

Except.

Inside.

Deep fucking inside.

The darkness threatens to sneak through and come out to play. And sometimes, just sometimes, I have to let the dark out to play. It's the right thing to do.

In so many ways not keeping it caged is correct—it helps me be the right type of man for Rose. Or so I believe.

It helps me to keep being the man she wants, no, deserves me to be at home. Keeps me being the father I should always be. Because they all have my fucking heart, every one of them holding onto pieces of it. No one else had a chance. I'm not even sure how it happened, Rose must have taken it that moment when we were sixteen years old. To be honest, I've never had a hold on it since that time.

And that's okay, I want it this way. She deserves it. If anyone can look after my heart, it's Rose. I would gladly pull out the one that beats in my chest and hand it to her, so she fully understands that it only beats for her. Just her. Without her, I'm a dead man walking.

"Not you." His words fail as his hands drop to his sides. He shakes his head, taking a large step back.

I can feel the disappointment that Rose will have, it leaks from me, but it doesn't stop me from what I'm about to do. It can't stop me.

"You shouldn't be here." He tries talking again.

The wind picks up and slaps across my face, my heavy black boots stay exactly where they are as I watch him. My right hand clenches the gun, the silencer already screwed into position.

"You stopped." He tries again, frantic now, especially because I don't respond to him. His eyes search past me, but there's no escape.

The girl behind him moves.

I thought she was dead, I guess I was wrong.

He looks back at her then quickly to me. "I found her like that. I swear it. You must believe me."

He's lying.

Fuck! He is so lying.

The girl comes around. She manages to sit up, her mouth moves to open in a scream, but I shake my head in warning as I watch her.

"Go," I yell.

She scrambles to her feet, but he steps in her way not letting her pass.

"You can't let her go and not me. I was only trying to help."

Tears fall from her eyes as he touches her midsection. She's scared of him. Frightened. Terrified. But most of all horrified as the gun in my hand rises.

His hand drops from her waist, and she runs, straight past me and out of the alleyway.

Now, it's just him and me.

My finger begs me to pull the trigger. To end it right now. Finish him.

He's sick. I watched as he struck the girl and dragged her down the alley as if she were nothing but a toy and he had every right to touch her.

He didn't.

She didn't give him that kind of permission.

Rose.

She pops into my head.

I shake my head.

Right now, I should be at home with her. In the same bed, snuggled up and kissing my way down her neck, pushing her long, beautiful blonde hair out of the way and curling it in my fingers as I pull her to me.

She likes it rough.

"Come on, man, we can work this out."

He snaps me out of my daze from the place I should be right now. Where my woman and kids sleep.

I should be here.

But this isn't his first time. A hit is a hit, no matter how hard someone tries to get out of it. Money's paid, and my job must be completed.

This creep's latest victim will now be his last.

And mine... well, he won't be my last. No matter how hard I try to tell myself otherwise.

"I can pay you. Double whatever someone else is." He bites his lip and looks down.

He's lying, he doesn't have any money. And it doesn't matter if he was the richest fucker on this earth, it's the first contract that's binding. You don't go back on your word. It's a code I live by, it's how my business has always worked. It's why I'm the best and why I'm sought after.

I don't even bother answering, just a simple shake of the head will suffice.

Sirens sound in the distance. Drunken partiers walk the streets. Not one of them looks down the alley. Why would they? It's dark. It's menacing. It's merely a gap between two old brick structures, a cold and uninviting place. Why would anyone even think to wander down here? And one thing you learn when growing up is never to go somewhere you can't be seen. People like me hide in murky, obscure places ready to murder them.

And we do. We annihilate whoever's in our contract. It's my job to make sure the execution is accomplished.

Correctly.

No fuss.

First time.

Just like John and me right now. Just like where he brings all his victims. Places no one else wants to go, so the screams are muffled, and her cries go unheard.

The realization hits him as he takes a deep breath. His eyes flutter closed, and he makes his move to get past me. But you don't get past me unless I let you. Him, I don't intend to allow.

His eyes register it before his body does. They go wide as my finger pulls back hard on the trigger. He drops to the ground. His hand lifting to cover his chest, which now has my bullet lodged inside. His eyes don't bother looking up to me. Why would they, he has mere minutes to live.

No one's going to save him.

Not in this life.

Taking a deep breath in as John takes his last one out, a smirk tugs at my lips while I turn and walk out of the alley.

I'm back...

2

ROSE

His hands wrap around my waist, the flutters that fly within my stomach since we first met have never left. His breath whispers on my neck, and all I want to do right now is let him tie me up and have his way with me. I know it's what he wants as well, but we can't.

Little Liam–well, not so little anymore–spots us, rolls his eyes as he walks into the kitchen then turns and walks out. "Do you really have to?" he asks as he retreats.

"Homework, Liam."

He shakes his head at my words while he continues walking out. Turning, so Liam's hands stay put on me, I lean up and kiss those lips, the same ones that have loved me non-stop for the last five years he's been back. Our kids are older, we are older. But our love, it's still new. How that's possible? I still don't know. It's not something I take for granted. I'm sure many loves aren't like ours, we're lucky. I don't know a single love story like ours.

Jake and Addy have both moved back and we're all close again. Having them both so near is a blessing as well. Little

Liam idolizes the ground Jake walks on. And to him, Addy's the prettiest woman he's ever seen.

"I want to push you over this bench and fuck you until you can no longer walk, Rose."

My face flushes as he pushes himself against me, hard. My first instinct is to push back on him, but he bites my neck while his hands roam everywhere they can touch until he finds my bare skin. He lifts my shirt to my bra.

"I wouldn't go in there, Dad's molesting Mom again."

Liam groans at little Liam's words. I push away, pulling my shirt down as Hayden steps in. He doesn't say much, just sits on the bench with his head hanging low as he reads something on his cell.

"Do you plan on saying hi?" I ask Hayden.

He lifts his head and stands. Walks around and kisses my cheek then sits back down. Hayden nods his head to Liam who's now leaning against the counter watching him.

"I'm moving out."

The cloth that was in my hand drops to the floor. Liam doesn't move, just watches Hayden as he looks up to us.

"No. I mean... are you sure?" I ask him. I've kept him as long as I could possibly keep him here. Protected him for even longer. I love him, even if biologically he isn't mine. He's mine in every other way.

"Sorry Mom, but think... you could finally turn that room into an office."

My head shakes fast. "That room will be yours... forever. It won't change, because you can always come back."

"Where do you think you're going?"

Shit! Hayden straightens in his seat. He also knows that voice and the meaning behind it. Liam isn't happy. Liam and Hayden, they're more alike than little Liam and Liam.

Hayden chose Liam, that's the difference. Where most saw the bad in Liam, Hayden saw the good.

"Moving in with Jake."

"Not happening."

Just then Jake walks in, helps himself to the fridge and turns to all of us.

There's silence.

Quiet.

You could hear a pin drop it's that still in here.

Jake's eyes land on Liam. If Liam had a gun in hand right now, Jake would run.

"It's not happening, sorry, kid," Jake says to Hayden then walks out, taking the beer he stole with him.

"Dad, fuck! Really? Did you have to do that?" Hayden swears.

"I did nothing."

It's true, Liam didn't. But he also did by his nonverbal response. He knows that his reaction is what caused Jake to change his mind.

"Isabelle's outside right now trying to kiss on a boy. Liam's addicted to YouTube videos. I'm a man now. You realize that. I have grown-ass men as friends, which Isabelle has tried to hang out with on multiple occasions. I *need* my space."

Liam chuckles at his words and shakes his head. Then stops as quickly as he started and pins Hayden with his eyes. "Where the fuck is she?"

Hayden points, Liam walks off.

"Mom." I don't want him to leave either, but he's right, he is an adult now. I've done the best I can keeping him here and safe.

"I'll talk to him. Maybe pack when he isn't here."

Hayden gets up, kisses my cheek, then leaves. He's

hardly home as it is. He works with Liam and Sax part-time while he goes to university. Hayden is Liam's favorite, we all know it. It's hard for Liam to comprehend that Hayden might not need him now.

"That girl."

"She's going through a stage," I say as Liam walks back in.

He shakes his head. "That stage better be finished soon, before I start distributing bullets to those boys."

I laugh at his words. "It's time. You have to let him go." Liam doesn't say anything to my words, so I continue, "He's still yours. He just needs... space. Give him that."

"You'll have to distract me," he says pushing against me. He opens the food pantry and pushes me in then shuts the door. His hands make fast work removing my top and then pulling my skirt all the way up so his hands can grab my ass. Pulling my G-string out of the way, he smiles.

"That, I can do." My lips touch Liam's as he slides into me. We've mastered the art of fucking hard and quiet. We've had to, he never stops. Ever.

"My fucking beautiful Rose." His words breathe life into me, each and every time. He distracts me with them, takes everything I am feeling.

He makes me focus on only one thing.

Him.

Liam Black is a master at fuckery, just like he's a master assassin.

And I know what he did last night.

I'm just waiting for him to tell me.

3

BLACK

"Where were you the other night? Or the last week to be exact? I've been covering for you, but even Hayden's noticing." I sit across from Sax, his hand rubbing over his bald head as he watches me while waiting for an answer.

"Busy."

"Don't bullshit me, Black. I know what you've been doing. What about John the other night? That mother who contacted us, you just happen to say no to her?"

"We get those calls all the time."

Sax nods his head. It's true. They ring and ask for protection, then they ask if we do extra. Killing. The answer is usually no, unless... well, unless I'm feeling extra twitchy.

"We do, and I know how much you hate to say no."

He's right. It's hard trying to find a new normal. I found it, but then slowly drifted back to my old kind of normal. This time though, I'm not alone. I have a family to consider, I have to think about them in all aspects of life.

"I was out."

He shakes his head. "You always seem to be out." He

pulls out a newspaper and throws it on the desk. John's face is plastered on the front cover. "Don't bullshit me. Fucking next time make the damn body disappear."

Just as he finishes talking, Hayden walks in. He's dressed much like me—in all black. He looks to Sax who nods his head then Hayden looks back to me.

"Shooting range?" Hayden asks. We go often. He's good, better than me.

"Not today," I say. He looks down, his face restrained, his hands glued to his side.

"A drink?" Hayden offers.

Sax kicks me under the table. "Sure."

Hayden walks off first, Sax shakes his head as I get up and follow him. Sax ended up buying his business in town. The bar is easy to get to as it's next door. I'm sure he did that on purpose, buying his business next door to some place that serves his favorite drinks.

"She's contacting me," are Hayden's first words as we walk out of the building. We aren't even inside the bar yet.

"Your mother," I reply.

She tried contacting Rose a few years back, we gave her more money and she went away. Of course, she's back, the money must have dried up.

Hayden nods his head. We don't make a move to go inside the bar—Sax suggested it so he could talk to me.

"She wants to try..." he looks down, "... so she says."

I have to bite my inner cheek to stop the expletives that want to rip from my mouth. His mother and stepfather are lowlife scum—actually that's being kind, more like fucking pond scum.

"You aren't going to say anything?" Hayden asks.

"I have nothing to say."

His fingers whip through his hair and his expression is

pained. "Dad, this is the one time I need you to tell me what to do."

"Not happening. You're old enough to figure what you want on your own."

"Is this payback? In your way this is retaliation for me wanting to leave, isn't it?"

"Wrong! This is me letting you be an adult. So be a fucking adult." My feet start walking before I say anything else. Hayden follows on behind me.

"If you don't tell me what I should do, I'll tell Mom what you've been doing late at night."

My feet come to a halt.

The curve of my mouth twitches.

"You don't want to hear my thoughts on those people, Hayden. Trust me. And don't think for a second you can tell Rose any-fucking-thing. It's not your place, so keep silent." My eyes bulge with anger as I clench my fists, the irritation is quite clear on my face.

A girl calls out Hayden's name. He looks over the street then back to me. "Are you going to ask me who that is?"

"No."

"Do you care?"

"Don't ask me questions you know the answer to. You aren't stupid. Don't act it." I can feel his stare on me as I turn and walk away. Getting into my truck I notice her, the girl who called out to him. She has her arms wrapped around his waist and is trying to kiss him. Hayden isn't letting her. He isn't even holding her. Instead, he's watching me closely.

"HEY, BLACK." Addy kisses me on the cheek before she walks out.

Jake's on the couch with a beer in hand watching some shit on the television. He's swearing, his nose is scrunched, and his lip is turned up. "Can you believe this shit?"

My legs go up on his coffee table and he turns fast, pushing them off.

"Fuck, man, you know she hates that shit. She's banned sex next time I let you put your damn feet up on her table." He starts wiping the table frantically then sits back on the couch. I know she hates it, it's the sole reason I do it. I like to stir him up, he does it enough to us.

"Oh, *come on*... you can't kill him. He's the fucking star."

"What the fuck is this shit?"

"Vikings," he says simply. He taps his braid in his hair and I laugh.

"Are you fucking joking?"

He shrugs his shoulders. "What can I say? The women love Ragnar. Addy likes to role play."

"You're trying to be a Viking?" I ask while shaking my head.

"I am a fucking Viking. Have you seen me?"

"Hayden's mom is back."

Jake's beer pauses at his mouth, he places it down and immediately switches the television off.

"Rose is Hayden's mom," he corrects me.

"You know what I fucking mean."

His head starts shaking. "No. No, I fucking don't. You mean that piece of trash wants more money. That's fucking it, isn't it? I'll kill the bitch myself."

"Sit the fuck down, you wanna be fucking Ragnar."

He huffs but listens.

"And if Isabelle decides to bring a boy back to the house one more fucking time, the next one will leave with a bullet in his leg." I have to remind myself he was a big part of the kid's life when I was away for years. They consider Jake their second father. To him, they're his as well. He and Addy don't have any kids, they're second parents to ours and good ones at that. That's the whole reason Hayden thought it would be a good idea to move in with him.

"Rose wasn't like that. She was reserved, different than other girls."

He coughs. "You knew her when she was whole, she broke after that. That's how you found her, remember? Broken. So maybe she was like Isabelle, screaming for attention."

"Isabelle won't be fucking broken."

He nods his head.

Addy walks in, stops, and stares at us.

"She's just being a teenager and exploring, leave her be." Then she's gone again, picking up her cell from the table as she goes.

Addy and Isabelle are close. She tells Addy things she won't tell Rose and me.

"Addy doesn't have to know if we shoot one of them."

Jake shrugs his shoulders nonchalantly switching the television back on.

4

ROSE

"They're currently discussing shooting the next boy she brings home," Addy says as she sits down. We live next door to each other, it's easy, and we've become like sisters. I never thought I'd be as close to someone as I am with Casey. But Addy was easy to get along with.

Little Liam steps in and walks straight into Addy's open arms. She squeezes him tight as he lays his head on her. He doesn't move, and I smile at the relationship they have. She chose not to adopt, she considers our kids hers as well. We're basically one big happy family, one I never really had.

"She's only doing it for attention," Little Liam grumbles into Addy's shoulder.

Addy smiles and I shake my head.

"She's a teenager. As long as she isn't being... silly. I guess." I shrug my shoulders.

What can I do? Ban her from boys? Yeah, that doesn't work. My mother tried the strict approach and that turned out terrible. So, I'm attempting a different method and hoping and praying it works.

"Dad's going to kill the next boy he busts her kissing." Little Liam laughs then walks back to his computer.

"Have you talked to him, yet?"

My hand stops the knife from cutting the apple I have in front of me as I look up to Addy. "What am I meant to say? Liam, are you back to being a hitman for Sax?"

I feel my mind and body deflate.

It's not something I want to think about, let alone relive.

"I asked Jake. Jake said he spoke to Sax. And Sax laughed. That he wouldn't allow him to do that."

My body relaxes. I'd seen some articles which reminded me of Liam's past. The smoothness of his kills. The people he assassinated. Same M.O. But he would only do that if Sax had asked him to do so. Not willingly. He left that life behind. He has this one with us, now.

"Thanks, Addy." I didn't ask her to ask Jake, but she did anyway. It's a relief because the only other person Liam is close to is Jake.

"So, what're the plans for Christmas? We doing it here again?" Addy asks.

I smile. Every year I throw a big Christmas party and invite around all our friends and family. We all wear green or white, and once the kids have eaten and settled, the adults drink. It's my favorite time of the year.

"We are."

Addy smiles at my answer. "And maybe now you won't be as stressed either. Especially because Black isn't doing the things you thought he was."

I shake my head, the smile not reaching my cheeks. "Maybe. It still doesn't explain where he's been going. Why I could smell gunpowder on him when he returned."

Addy stands up and walks over to me. Her hand touches

my shoulder and she pulls me in for a hug. Her hands wrap around me tightly as she tries to soothe me. "He's been good for years. Well, not good, but Black good... if you know what I mean." She chuckles while pulling back and kisses my cheek.

"He has, hasn't he?" As the words leave my mouth, Liam walks in. He comes straight to me, just like he does every time he enters our house, and his hands wrap around my center, pulling me back to him.

"This day needs to end... with you in bed and me on top of you," he whispers in my ear so no one can hear. I nod to his words.

Hayden walks in with a bottle of beer in one hand and his face strained.

"Why are you drunk?" Liam asks as his hold digs harder on my hips. Hayden puts the beer to his lips and takes a long drink. He finishes the bottle and places it on the bench, then he looks past me to Liam. His expression is pained and angry. Looking at Liam, I notice his usual expression on his face, but the slight flutter of his lashes is a tell I've come to know. He's angry but not showing it.

"What's going on here?" I snap, stepping out of Liam's grasp. He reaches for me but I don't let him pull me back. Jake sits down next to Addy, and they say nothing while they wait for someone to answer me. Both refuse. "One of you better answer me, *right now*."

"Why don't you tell her, Dad?" Hayden's voice is full of venom. I look back to Liam who has his arms crossed over his chest as he watches his son, Hayden.

"Nothing to speak about. Maybe you should go and cool down?"

Hayden walks to the fridge and grabs another beer. Jake makes a move to stop him, but halts when I step up to him and take it from his hands. Hayden doesn't say a word just leans against the fridge.

"Someone better start speaking... *now.*" Looking between Hayden and Liam, both don't say a word, so I look at Jake, and he sighs heavily.

"Hayden's mother's back."

"Rose is his mother," Addy interjects.

Everyone goes silent.

"Oh..." Addy looks down awkwardly.

My heart beats hard in my chest. That woman isn't his mother, she isn't even a good person. The way they used to treat Hayden as if he was their slave. Someone they could beat up on when they felt angry. Starve. Neglect. They didn't deserve him.

"Mom."

My head starts shaking. I look back to Liam, who's watching, assessing me for a reaction.

Liam waits before he speaks to see where I am at. "It means nothing."

Liam's lying.

Turning away fast and back to Hayden who's no longer leaning on the fridge, he's staring at me.

"You want to get to know her?" I ask because I know it's true. His eyes are glassy as he nods his head once.

I can feel it—my heart breaking.

That bitch doesn't deserve him.

At all.

Liam reaches for me, but I push his hand away and turn to him. "You didn't tell me?"

"It's stupid. She isn't his mother, you are." Liam looks past me to Hayden. "Isn't she, Hayden?"

"You know you are. No one can replace you, Mom."

I get looks when I go out with Hayden. I'm too young to

have him, but that doesn't bother me, never has and never will.

"You should if that's what you want. We should all meet her. I would like to."

Hayden opens his mouth, then shuts it.

"If you give her a cent of your money, I'll kill you myself," Jake speaks. He gets up and walks out with Addy, not saying goodbye. Leaving just the three of us in the kitchen.

"She hasn't asked for money, Mom."

Pulling him into my arms, I hug him. The thought that someone could come in and make him love them more than me—it hurts. The ache in my heart is real, I'm not going to lie. But I'll also respect whatever it is he wants to do. He's an adult now. We have to start letting him be one without us constantly being there for him. And that's a hard pill to swallow, especially for Liam. If he had his way, Hayden would stay under his nose forever.

"As long as she doesn't hurt you, that's all I care about." Letting him go, he walks out of the room. Turning to Liam, I walk up to him and hit his hands away as he tries to pull me to him. He doesn't look shocked.

"Secrets! Don't fucking keep them from me, Liam Black. I mean it. He's mine as much as he's yours."

"No secrets," he says to me. Liam steps closer, places his hand on my hip slowly, but not pulling me to him. He leans in, his lips touch mine as he talks into them. "My Rose... I shall love you forever, in this life and the next."

My heart melts like putty, just as it does in his hands every single damn time.

Putty meet Black. Liam Black.

5

BLACK

Secrets. I promised not to keep them. And not telling her everything is killing me. But it would upset her more if she knew. It also scares me what she might do if she found out.

"You're up early." Isabella sits down next to me. She's grown so much. I never thought I'd have kids let alone raise a girl.

I know nothing about girls.

Correction, I didn't.

Until her.

I've learned she's cranky when it's that time of the month, and that chocolate is her favorite food during that time. And that I'm also classed as evil when I tell her no to going out late at night with her deadbeat friends. And by that, I mean boys in particular.

"Taking you to school, Mom's sleeping in.

Rose was up all night preparing food for Hayden's so-called mother to come over tonight for dinner.

"I can walk to school."

I shake my head. "Not happening." She slumps in her

seat, her head leaning on my shoulder. Despite her cry out for attention with those god-awful boys she wants to date, she's a good kid. Compassionate. Great with her brother. When she isn't mad at him for talking to her friends.

"Are you wearing black to the dance?" she asks taking my coffee cup from my hand and drinking it.

"Yes."

The father-daughter dance is this weekend. It took some convincing. Well, no, I should say Rose talked me into it. Or fucked me into it.

"Can I wear black, too? We can match."

"Sounds good," I say taking the mug from her hands.

She pulls her bag over her shoulder as she stands. "Wear a pink tie."

The liquid in my mouth blurts out. Isabelle laughs as she walks to the door.

What is with these women in my life and the color pink?

"SHE'LL ASK me if you're working tonight, what am I meant to say?" Sax asks as we walk out of the office. He's going to pick up Casey and their daughter over at mine. I don't want to be there, I don't want to meet Hayden's biological mother tonight. That house is the furthest I want to be away from. I met her once when I got those scum to sign the papers for Hayden. Never again. That bitch doesn't care. She's only there for the money. And it's me that's going to have to put Hayden back together when she breaks him, just like she used to do when he was a kid.

"Tell her I'm with a client tonight and couldn't leave."

He shakes his head. "You're really putting me in a shit position, Black, really fucking shit."

"Goodnight."

Sax shakes his head as he drives off. Rose was up all night preparing the food and the house for Hayden's mother's arrival. I couldn't care less. Instead, I'm going to do something useful, I'm going to fucking work.

Driving to a local bar I see him through the window. He's talking to a young man, way too young for him to be linked to. My hand twitches on the gun under my seat. The silencer already in place.

Before I step out, the young boy turns around. My heart stops. My feet start moving before I can stop and I'm running straight into the bar. My hands grab the back of the man's neck, pulling him from his seat and throwing the fucker to the floor.

Hayden looks at me glassy-eyed with no idea what's happening.

"Daddd," he slurs. His eyes are bloodshot.

Looking at the man who's now scrambling to his feet, I ask, "What did you give him?"

His head starts shaking. "Nothing." The lie leaves his mouth and sends a stink through the room.

Hayden tries to stand, but fails and falls back into the chair he was sitting in. Pulling the man to me by the collar, I push the gun into his abdomen.

"You have two seconds to tell me what you gave my son before my finger gets trigger-happy and puts a bullet right into your belly."

"Just something to make him happy."

Pushing him away I don't kill him there and then, but make no mistake I will. Just not right now while everyone's watching. Pulling Hayden to me, he falls, hardly being able to stand. The bartender looks to us, unsure of what to do. I shake my head and carry

Hayden out to the car. He falls in easily, moaning as he does.

Looking back, the man's starting his sports car and he drives off.

I'll kill that bastard tomorrow.

Or maybe tonight.

"Daddd... I didn't mean to."

I don't answer him as we drive home. Rose is standing out the front, her cell phone to her ear when I pull up. She's dressed in a black dress that hugs her curves nicely, but there's a look of worry etched on her beautiful face. She runs to the car, hanging up her cell when she sees me, and goes straight to the passenger door. Rose's hands touch Hayden's face, she's checking to see he's okay.

Her eyes fall on me. "What happened? Tell me what's wrong with him?"

Hayden reaches out and touches Rose's cheek, stroking it softly. She just cups his hand and allows him to continue.

"Take him inside. I have somewhere to be."

Rose's perfect blue eyes go large, her hand squeezes Hayden's hard. "Did someone do this?"

Turning the engine on, I rev it, waiting for them to get out of the way.

"No. No, you aren't going anywhere, Liam Black. Get out of this car right now and help me get our son inside."

My hands squeeze the steering wheel. I want to kill him. Agonizingly slowly. Painfully.

"Liam, I need you."

Hayden's head falls on Rose's shoulder while he stays in the car. His eyes are heavy and he's falling asleep. Cutting the engine at her words, I get out and walk around, pushing Rose out of the way, and grab hold of Hayden. He's large, almost the same size as me, and he's full of muscle.

"Fuck."

Isabelle walks out the door.

That's when I see her, Hayden's biological mother, she's watching us. She doesn't seem concerned that her son isn't in any sort of state of coherence.

"Is he going to be okay? Tell me he's going to be okay?" Rose mutters walking behind me. Hayden's biological mother doesn't say a word. She just looks at me, and I know in that moment she isn't here to see him. She's here to see what she can get out of him, or should I say us.

"Leave." My voice is harsh, and she flinches at my words as I walk in away from her. I hear Rose offering an apology.

"I'm sorry, Sandy, tonight isn't going to work." Then I hear the click of the door before Rose is behind me as I lay Hayden on his bed. Pulling her to me, she starts crying as we look down on him.

"I'll get you a blanket."

She nods her head into my shoulder as she sits down on the sofa in Hayden's room. Many nights when he was sick she would sit on that very sofa all night to watch him. She's done it with all the kids. But tonight's different. Fear is evident in her eyes.

6

ROSE

He doesn't stir all night, several times I have to check to ensure he's still breathing. I'm dressed in my black dress and haven't moved. Liam comes in several times bringing me a coffee or just to check on me. I can feel his anger and his need for revenge leaching from every single pore in his body. But I don't want him to leave, I don't want him to go down that path. I thought he had gone down it once before and I can't risk him actually succeeding this time. Last time it took him away from me for five, long and painful years, he missed all of little Liam's milestones. Risking something like that would kill me. This time for sure.

"Mom." Hayden sits up, and my legs automatically take me to a standing position to move closer to him to make sure he's okay. "I'm fine, Mom."

I shake my head as he pushes my hand away. "What happened, Hayden? I was so worried."

He grabs the bottle of water next to the bed and drinks it before he answers. "I was nervous, about how Dad would handle it. I went for a drink... then, nothing. It's all just sort of blank."

"You were drugged, Liam found you."

"Dad saw?" I nod my head. One thing Hayden never wants to do is disappoint anyone. It's just who he is, around us at least.

"What did he do?" The other kids don't know much about what Liam does, or has done. Hayden, though, he knows it all.

"Nothing. He brought you home."

He shakes his head and attempts to stand, then sits back down when his head spins. "And, did she come?"

I nod my head slowly. "She did."

A look of pain comes over him. "She saw, didn't she?"

"It doesn't matter what she saw. Hayden, you need to rest. How about a shower and some breakfast?"

"Where's Dad?"

Looking over my shoulder, I can see Liam in the kitchen. He's watching us, waiting for us to come out. He knows Hayden's awake.

Before I can say anything, the bedroom door is pushed all the way to the wall as Jake walks in. Anger written all over his face. "What the fuck were you thinking? You know not to accept drinks from strangers. What the actual fuck, Hayden. I know you've become accustomed to the bad guy routine since you're used to us scary motherfuckers. That doesn't mean you should let your damn guard down." Jake steps forward, grabs hold of Hayden's head with both hands and pushes it. "You need to think with this... all the fucking time. How do you think your dad stayed alive for so fucking long? Hey? Because he's one smart motherfucker."

"Jake," Liam calls out.

Jake stops talking and walks straight out of the room.

Hayden hangs his head.

"It's because they care."

"I fucked up, Mom. I knew something was off with that man. I was on edge."

My arms wrap around him tightly. Jake and Liam are talking softly in the kitchen. Pulling away and shutting Hayden's door behind me they both go quiet when I reach them.

"Addy's waiting for me," Jake says then quickly tries to escape.

"You'll stop him, won't you, Jake?" I can't see Jake as my eyes are trained on Liam. But I hear his footsteps come to a halt.

Liam shakes his head at me. "Jake can't stop me from doing anything," Liam says watching me.

Jake's footsteps start again and I know he's walking out.

"It's almost Christmas, Liam. I want this year to be perfect. Hayden's leaving, it's our last one with him living here. The kids are growing so quickly. Soon they will want to spend more time with their friends than us. So stop this madness, because I know what you're thinking, I know what you want to do. You want to harm that man who hurt your child. And even if I do as well, I won't, because that's not the way the world goes. It's not what a normal person does." My breathing's harsh as I stare at him.

"I'm not normal."

My head starts shaking. "That's all you got from that conversation?" My eyebrow raises in question.

"Mom." Spinning around, I see Hayden standing at his door. His eyes flicking from me to Liam. "Sandy wants to come around for Christmas."

"Ummm... okay. Is that something you want?"

Hayden's eyes flick to Liam again. Turning around,

Liam's watching Hayden with intent. "Stop it." Liam looks to me. "Stop that. I know what you're doing. Stop it."

Liam places his coffee mug down and calls out Isabelle's name. She comes running ready to go to the movies as Liam grabs his keys and walks straight past us and out the door without saying another word.

"He doesn't mean to do it," Hayden says. His muscles in his arms bulge and I realize he isn't my little Hayden anymore. It's hard to let them go. Even harder when it's the exact moment you realize it. "He's come a long way," Hayden says dropping his hand from rubbing his jaw. I walk up to him, touching his face.

"So have you, and no going back."

He nods, agreeing. "There's someone else..."

"Hayden?" I ask in question.

"I want you to meet her. Today."

"Liam?" I ask, but he shakes his head.

"He would scare her, she doesn't understand him."

I nod. Many people walk the other way when they see him coming toward them. His reputation is still intact, even if he isn't the killing machine he once was.

"Are you up to that? You need to rest."

"I'm fine, Mom." He turns walking back to his room, stops with his hand on the door and looks back. "Thank you, Mom."

I smile, the tears threatening to leave my eyes. When he closes his bedroom door the tears drop.

7

BLACK

M y foot taps impatiently as I wait out the front in my car.

I've tracked him down.

Gotten as much info on him as possible.

NAME: George Cunner

Age: Fifty-two

Occupation: Trauma doctor

Other Details: One kid. No wife. Presumed to like young boys. No sufficient evidence.

HE'S A DOCTOR—THAT made me cringe. This man who drugged my son is a damn doctor, someone who's meant to help people. He's actually someone who has too much time and money on his hands and has decided to drug and potentially rape boys. That's the sole reason I was onto him in the first place. A mother suspected and wanted him gone. Her son—the same age as Isabelle—was treated by Dr.

Cunner. Woke up with his pants undone, and Dr. Cunner doing his up. No evidence was found of foul play, but the boy knew he did something. It happened on more than one occasion.

The hit was made.

The money paid.

And I can honestly say this one *will* make me undeniably happy. To take someone like him from this world, maybe with a little torture to begin with, I live for that shit.

His house is over the top. It screams money, so much so it's ostentatious. That's the only word for it. From the BMW sitting in front to the perfect lawns and the size of the house, it's certainly grandiose. I notice him through the window, sitting in a large wingback chair with not a clue in the world that I'm watching his every move. Not a hint I've come to end his life. And the one thing that ticks me the most—no remorse for what he did last night.

My cell starts ringing, and Rose's face flashes on the screen. It's been a few hours and I haven't ventured back to the house. Seeing Hayden in that state made my blood boil. Jake wanted to be with me to end Cunner's life. But that victory lies solely within me. I'm not even doing it for the money. No. That money will be sent back. I'm doing this for me. And Hayden.

"Rose."

"He's got a girlfriend, and she's sweet, Liam. I think he loves her. Maybe. He brought her around today. Wanted me to meet her. A girlfriend."

"Uh-huh."

"You can't scare her, he's afraid you'll scare her. Try to smile when he tells you about her. Try to smile when you meet her." Turning away from Cunner I get back into my car while I listen. "Actually, don't smile, your forced smiles come off as serial-killer like."

"I would lean towards hitman."

"You used to be..." she says quietly.

"Yes," I answer her back.

"You'll come back tonight, won't you? You aren't working late? I need you, Liam Black. I need you, now." The car starts before the last word leaves her mouth.

"I'm coming." I hang up, looking up one last time and seeing him sitting exactly where he was, not moving watching television.

Scum like him should die slowly.

And he will.

BEFORE I EVEN GET IN the front door, her hands are on me. She pulls me in, tearing at my shirt as I kick the door shut. Pulling her to me her lips slam on mine, then she talks into my lips. "Jake has the kids." I smirk on her lips and pick her up by her ass. She giggles and her lips leave mine. She leans back tearing her shirt from her body, exposing herself. My lips beg to bite her nipples.

Her hands stop me by grabbing my face and lifting my head as we reach our room. "Tell me you love me, Liam Black." Placing her on the bed, she wiggles free from her shorts so she lies in front of me completely naked.

All fucking mine.

Mine.

My head screams.

My fingers touch the inside of her calf, slowly dragging my fingertips up until I reach her inner thigh. She takes a deep breath letting it go slowly. Her eyes scream lust, her hands stay at her side careful not to move as I track my way up her body.

As I reach her sweet pussy, she flinches from anticipation. Leaning down, my breath touches her inner thigh.

"You have too many clothes on," she mutters.

"You have just the right amount off." She laughs at my words. She's naked and perfect. In every way. My tongue licks high on her inner thigh. Her breathing becomes even deeper.

"Liam."

"Rose," I say then kiss the other thigh, licking my way up and lifting as I get to where she wants me to be.

"Stop teasing me, Liam Black."

I chuckle at her. Then give her what she wants—my mouth on her pussy. Her hands come to my hair and she doesn't dictate where she wants me. She holds on, combing her fingers through it, as I take from her all she will give. Inserting two fingers, she clenches hard around them. The power I have over her is enticing. But the power she has over me is the most addictive drug on this planet.

I often wonder if others feel the same way we do. Feeling like we are made for each other and her love knows no bounds. She loves with all she is, and I take it like the selfish prick I am. Because I want it. I want all she is—every breath, her very life. I want her. I choose her.

She comes on my fingers. Pushing me away she tells me to undress. "Too many clothes," she says. She's right. But her pleasure is my first priority. Always has been and always will be. I'm hard. Have been straining in my fucking trousers since I saw her waiting at the door for me. It's what she does even after all this time. That attraction will never change.

She watches me as if she's eagerly waiting for her next

meal, that I am the last meal she will ever eat. And I am, I will be her last. In this life and the next.

Climbing up the bed, she wraps her legs around me as I hover over her. Her hand slides between us, she grabs hold of my cock and inserts it herself. Straight into her wet fucking pussy. She moans loudly, her hand coming up and gripping my back.

One movement inside of her, and I'm fucking done. I become something that's so hungry for it, I'm a starving animal. And it's all I need to survive. She's all I fucking need to survive.

She screams my name as I fuck her, as I take everything. Her nails dig into my back, hard. She's angry. *How did I not notice that before?* Because I was so fucking invested in all things Rose and I in this bed right now, I didn't notice.

Pulling out of her and standing, she shakes her head.

She now realizes I know. She turns and gets on all fours. Taking her hips, I do what any fucking man would do to the woman they crave, love, admire, want. I pull her to me, hard, and slide straight in. Then I fuck her until we can both no longer talk, let alone move.

8

ROSE

I've been watching him sleep. Liam's hand lays possessively on my stomach, as his head faces toward me while he lays on his belly. He's still naked, lying there in all his perfect glory.

"Go to sleep." He pulls me closer, so our bodies are touching again. My pussy's sore. He didn't stop at one, no, we then went to the shower then back to the bed. And now I can't stop thinking about Christmas Day.

"It has to be perfect. I want it to be perfect."

Liam grumbles next to me, laying his head on my boobs, kissing them softly before he answers me. "It will be. Everything you do is perfect."

Sometimes, just sometimes the words that leave his mouth knock me back. He puts so much thought into his words. He doesn't just share them with anyone. They are given, and if you're lucky to receive them then you're fortunate to know him. He doesn't even think when he says them to me. They mean so much. Lifting his arm off me, I climb onto his back and lie on him, he smirks with his eyes still closed as I kiss his back. He's naked, I'm naked and I'm sore, but touching him seems to make it go away.

"You make me so happy," I say kissing his back. "Never change, Liam."

He shakes his head, his smirk still in place. "I can feel your pussy on my back. Now I'm getting hungry again." He turns, flipping me, making me giggle.

"Mom, Isabelle's being a cow."

He stops and pulls the blanket up fast to cover us just as little Liam walks in. It's always him catching us in ways he shouldn't. He groans about it every chance he gets. But I'm never going to complain about Liam having his hands on me, it's one of my favorite things.

"Really?" Little Liam slams the door walking out.

Getting free from Liam's grasp, I get up, throwing on my silk robe. Liam's already up sliding on his trousers as he goes to the door. He looks back to me before he opens it. "Get back in bed. Naked. We have plans for today..." he grins, "... to do nothing but fuck." He walks out shutting the door behind him.

See what I mean? Sweet words.

It didn't last. Isabelle came back, and Liam was angry that she followed him. And Hayden ended up coming home, this time with his girlfriend, Miranda. Liam hasn't met her yet, and to be honest, I wasn't sure if Hayden was ready for that. But apparently, he is. Liam's cooking in the kitchen when Miranda comes over and says hello. Hayden grips her hip as if she needs him to stand. She's quiet, much like Hayden if you don't know him.

"Dad."

"Liam."

Hayden and I both call him at the same time. He comes out with tongs in hand as he stares at us, then to Miranda who looks up once then back to the floor.

"This is Miranda." Hayden doesn't let go of her. She looks up offering him a small smile. She has a short pixie hairstyle and she's tinier than me. Almost the same size as Isabelle.

"Hi, sir."

Liam nods to her, then turns and walks back into the kitchen.

Hayden looks disappointed.

"Staying for dinner?" Liam asks.

Hayden's frown turns into a small smile. "We are."

"Hayden... Mom and Dad were doing it again. Kicking us out and getting naked."

Hayden ruffles little Liam's hair, who's currently trying to grow it like Hayden's. "Next time, stay out." He winks and Miranda blushes next to him. She places her hand on his chest and looks up at him. The way she looks at him I can see it, she loves him very much. Looking at Hayden, I'm not sure he loves her in the same way.

"So good to see you again, Miranda," I tell her. She smiles, staying glued to Hayden. "Hayden, why don't you go and help your dad. Miranda can help me set up."

He pulls away from her, and her eyes linger as Hayden walks away.

"You really like him?" I question, starting to set the table.

Her eyes leave him, as she looks at me. "Very much so."

"He's a good kid."

"He's quiet, he thinks before he speaks. I like that about him. Most boys just try to sleep with you, Hayden isn't like that." I want to correct her, that Hayden is a man and that he is like that. Well, was. I've known of some of his girls. They've come here begging to see him. He's the ladies' man, which makes Jake extremely happy. Not so much, Liam, he hated that girls would come over for study dates. They talked too much and wouldn't leave. But Hayden hasn't brought any girls here for a long time. Not since he started university. We assumed he's been too busy with work and his studies, but maybe we were wrong.

"That's nice," I say. She sits at the table, folding the napkins. "If you'll excuse me."

Miranda nods her head lost in her own thoughts. Walking into the kitchen, I find Liam and Hayden laughing at something. Liam knows I'm there before Hayden, and he turns around, leans down and kisses me on the lips before he goes back to cooking.

"She's very smitten with you. Do you love her?"

Hayden looks past me to where she's sitting. "Not in the way she loves me." His honesty is brutal, it's one of my favorite traits about him. "But maybe I will."

"Maybe..." I answer him. Liam listens but doesn't say a word. He stopped stirring though, so I know he's listening.

"Isabelle is about to arrive home. Do you want to leave her alone with Miranda? Maybe you should go and hide her first."

He chuckles under his breath knowing full well what his sister is like. She's loud, obnoxious, and where she gets that from we don't know. Liam likes to blame Jake.

"Speaking of Isabelle, are you ready for tomorrow?"

Liam groans turning to me. His hands pull at my waist so I slam into him. "If I have to wear pink, I'm not going."

I laugh at him. "She wants to wear your color anyway."

"Good." He looks past me. "You don't think it's serious?" he asks.

I shake my head. "I think it's the most serious he's been with a girl, but I don't think it's what she's hoping for. She's smitten with him." He nods his head. "She's coming for Christmas, too."

"What happened to just us and family?"

"My mother will still be away on her cruise."

"There is a god."

I hit him in the chest while laughing. She can be too much sometimes. We're close now, but Liam sometimes can't handle her.

"Be nice tonight, all right? It's you he wants approval from. No one else."

Jake and Addy walk in. Liam rolls his eyes and lets me go.

"Who's the pixie Isabelle's currently talking to?" Jake asks.

Liam laughs as I groan while heading off to rescue Miranda from Isabelle. No one is good enough for Hayden. Hayden to Isabelle—he's almost superhero status.

9

BLACK

"It's too tight." Groaning, I pull at the tie. Rose fusses with it to make it looser. Then distracts me when her hands drop lower and cups my cock.

"If you're a good boy you might get a treat when you get home." She winks, and I stare.

"Did you just talk to me as if I were a dog?" Her hand drops and her eyes widen. "I'm just going to have to fuck you like one in that case," I say, grabbing her and spinning her around slapping her ass. She laughs and stands up, pulling her dress down which has risen up.

"She's nervous. Be good. Please."

I kiss her lips. "I'm always good."

Isabelle opens the door. These kids really need to learn to stop doing that. Boundaries need to be taught. Several times they've caught us, but that doesn't seem to deter them from barging in.

"Gross. Dad, you ready?"

She looks beautiful. Much like her mother. Her long blonde hair cascades down in curls over her sparkling black dress. She has on heels that make her come up to my shoulder in height.

"You look as beautiful as your mother." Her cheeks blush. "You always do, but tonight you remind me of her even more so. You just don't have a red dress on."

Rose grips my hip, remembering that night many years ago when I found her again and she was dressed in red. She is, and always will be, the prettiest woman I've ever seen.

"Thanks, Dad." She falls into my chest, hugging me tightly. Rose is crying behind me. She pulls at Isabelle and hugs her daughter. They've come a long way from where they started.

"Where's my girls at," Jake's voice booms through the house.

Rose lets go of Isabelle as Jake steals her.

"Don't scare all the boys, okay?" Rose whispers to me as she reaches up, her lips touching mine. I want to take her right now, have my way with her. She stopped me from doing what I need to do for the last few days.

"I'll do my best."

She rolls her eyes at me.

"YOU CAN GO, Dad. I'm going to hang with Sebastian."

I've been here for two hours and counting. There are only so many times you can dance when you don't know how to fucking dance. My eyes scan the room until they land on Sebastian. As soon as I find him his eyes avert to the floor.

"Stop it," Isabelle says nudging me with her arm.

"Your mother wants you home by eleven. Don't be late. Or Sebastian may lose an arm." Isabelle doesn't take my threats seriously, she just waves at me as she walks away over to the blond-haired punk of a kid.

Tearing my tie off as I go, a mother who was in there chaperoning stops me. Her hand touches my arm, squeezing. My eyes follow her hand then they track up to the lady whose hand is still currently on me.

"Oh, sorry." She drops her hand, fast. It touches her sides as she looks at me. "I'm Sebastian's mother, I just wanted to introduce myself properly. I see your daughter has a thing for him."

Her words are full of shit. She doesn't know Isabelle and who she has a thing for. Knowing Isabelle, this will last a month tops before she moves on. She's happy to do that, leave hearts broken in her wake. Which doesn't bother me at all. As long as she's safe.

"Okay, so I'm Alana. I know the kids are on Christmas break now, but I was wondering if it would be okay to maybe have a meet-up. They seem to be getting pretty serious. Your daughter is quite the little hussy, isn't she?"

I look back to my truck, it's begging for me to leave and not speak to this woman. She leans into me. Her hand touches my shoulder like that's any better than touching my arm without my permission. Shrugging she drops it, smiles softly and looks down.

"You don't talk much, do you?" She steps in closer to me. Now her body is directly in front of mine. "Must be hard raising a teenage girl all by yourself." She goes to touch me again, but I step back because hitting a woman is not what I do.

Killing them?

Fuck!

No, I don't do that either.

"I'm not by myself. Now, excuse me."

She steps in front of me, stopping me from going any further. I try to sidestep her, but this bitch is determined. And is now pissing me right off.

"I'll need your number, you know... to have that meet-up."

I shake my head.

"I'm sure your child has Isabelle's number."

Her head drops to the side like she's assessing me. I manage to step around her before she can step in my way again, and slide into the truck. Looking back through the rearview mirror as I drive off, I see her watching me. And I wonder how many other men she has tried to get her claws into.

Before I go home, I'm turning the wheel, taking myself to a place I know I should be. A place where a man should *not* still be breathing.

Cunner's seated precisely where he was last time in his wingback chair. This time though, he isn't watching television. He's pulling shoes on, then knots his tie as he gets ready. I watch him as he walks to his car, the BMW that proves he has more money than brains. I stay far back behind him as he drives off, and follow him all the way to a bar not too far from the first one I saw him at. My cell starts ringing as he walks through the door. He doesn't check his surroundings, he's not worried about anything. I'm not sure if that makes me even angrier, considering the kind of scum he is. He should be healing, after all, he is a damn doctor, but people must be wearing rose-colored glasses.

My cell stops and rings again.

Rose's name flashes on the screen. Putting the cell phone to my ear, she speaks without any words from me. "You left the dance an hour ago. Where are you?" My eyes follow

Cunner as he walks into the bar. I watch him nod his head to the man sitting next to him through the window.

"I'm driving home now."

"Liam..."

"I'll see you soon." Hanging up the phone, it's now two nights where I've left him breathing.

The next time... he won't be so lucky.

10

ROSE

Liam's tie is removed and bunched up in his hand as he walks in the door. His eyes are green and strong as they watch me.

"Isabelle called, told me you spoke to Sebastian's mother and said it was fine for her to go home with them?"

"I did no such thing."

"I know, that's why I asked for her to come straight home. She should be here any second."

Liam starts removing his jacket. And I have to contain my instincts to touch him. To be with him. He was out longer than he should have been. Usually, that wouldn't worry me. But I know Black, know him better than almost anyone on this planet. And something's been off, I can feel it. He's hiding something, it may not be big, except Black never hides anything from me. Ever.

"Now where were you, Liam?"

"Took a drive."

That's a half-truth, I can feel it. He definitely isn't telling me something.

"If you're not going to tell me the truth, it's best you sleep on the couch."

He steps toward me, and I step back, so his hands can't touch me. But he's too fast. His hands clasp on my back pulling me to him.

"I'll sleep with you because what I said is the truth. I was out in my car the whole time." His chest is in my face. Looking up to his eyes, green as the winter paddocks, they stare back at me with such intensity that I almost have to look away.

"You were in your car, the whole time?"

He nods his head.

Confirmation.

My heart settles as I fall into his embrace.

"And I take it you met Alana, Sebastian's mother?" I ask him, remembering the way Jake described her as a leech, and I laugh.

"You've met her?" he asks.

"Jake has," I answer as he smirks.

"I bet that would have been interesting." His hands start moving down my back until he reaches my ass. He picks me up, my legs wrap around him automatically. The front door opens and Isabelle walks in. I point to her room and she rolls her eyes. Liam carries me all the way to the bedroom. And I let him do whatever it is he wants to me, for the Christmas spirit and all. Let's face it, I am a giver.

I INVITED Sebastian's mother around. She actually insisted on coming over and discussing our children. Liam tried to get out of it. Insisted he needed to be elsewhere. That isn't happening, he isn't leaving me by myself to deal with meeting the parents of Isabelle's boyfriend. The knock comes on the door as Liam sits down at the table, placing the bread rolls in the middle. Isabelle beats me to the door, and I smile as Sebastian greets us, along with his mother. She's dressed in a short pink shirt, her belly and boobs out on display. I try to not stare. Really. Or even judge. She can wear what she wants, who am I to tell her otherwise.

"Thanks so much for having us, I figured it was time we all met."

I nod, but she kind of insisted on it. Didn't really give me a chance to say no. She steps into the house without me even saying she can. Looking around, her eyes land on Liam, and she stops. She offers him a small wave before she walks over to him and sits right next to him. He looks at her like she has a second head, her hand touches his shoulder, and I see the restraint he's holding onto by telling her not to touch him. Liam Black doesn't like to be touched, especially by those he doesn't know.

"Alana, isn't it?" I ask while shutting the door and then walking over to her. She looks at me, her smile as fake as her tits. She sits back, removing her hand from Liam's shoulder.

"Yes, and you're Lily?"

Liam looks up, waiting to see what I say.

"Rose."

"Oh, that's right. I knew it was a flower of some sort."

Liam coughs next to her, knowing full well she knew my name.

"So, you wanted to talk about our kids?"

Alana looks back to Liam, smiles then gazes back at me. "Yes, your daughter is quite the little man stealer. She has my Sebastian wrapped around her finger."

Liam looks past me, and I know the kids just walked in. Turning, I smile to Isabelle.

"Food's ready, how about you two go and grab it."

Isabelle nods, pulling a clueless Sebastian with her.

"I'm going to be straight with you, Alana. Okay?"

She nods her head, sits back and smiles at Liam again. Her hand goes to touch his shoulder, but he manages to move just in time.

"Isabelle won't be staying at your house. Don't ask her to again. She isn't a hussy as you so kindly put it the other night to her father. Who I might add, really doesn't like you touching him."

She looks to Liam, then back to me. "I never—" she goes to say but I hold up my hand, stopping her. Isabelle told me how Alana told her to lie to me and say she'd be at a friend's house. Liam told me about her and her words, and the way she attempted to get close to him. Before she can finish her sentence, the kids walk out.

Sebastian seems like a good kid. Despite his mother.

"Is your father around?" I ask Sebastian as he sits. He looks to his mother who crosses her arms over chest.

"Yes, but I don't allow him to see him," she replies for her son.

"Oh."

"He's a doctor and not a very good one. He should be fired." Sebastian doesn't say a word, just looks down to his plate as Isabelle serves him. "I'm not even sure how he has a license or what I saw in him," she continues on.

"What's your surname?" Liam asks Sebastian, who straightens in his chair at the voice of Liam.

"Cunner, sir," Sebastian answers.

I look to Liam who's suddenly gone very quiet. Placing my hand on his leg he matches mine with his. Hayden walks in, looks around the table and sits.

Alana who doesn't know any better leans over to him and introduces herself.

Throwing her out of my house wouldn't be acceptable, so I bite my lip in an attempt to stop myself. Thankfully my boys know better. Hayden doesn't speak to Alana, only offers a small smile before he looks to Sebastian. Liam drops my hand and gets up. His lips touch my neck and before I can say anything, he has his keys and he's gone.

Leaving us sitting there wondering why he left.

11

BLACK

I can't wait a day longer, it has to happen now. He's snuck into my life like a snake slithers into a hole. And what do you do with an unwanted guest? You remove it. He's exactly where I left him, sitting at the bar. By himself. The good doctor must be well and truly intoxicated by now. My hands grip the steering wheel and my heart accelerates as I watch him finally walk out. Excitement fills me, need fills me even more. The thing you were born to do shouldn't be a crime, right? I was born to do this. That was proven a long time ago when I took my first life.

Following him back to his place, I don't stay in my truck this time, and I've parked where no one can see me. My boots hit the asphalt and my hand squeezes tightly on the gun in my hand.

It used to be easy.

I didn't have to think about what I was going to do.

I just did it.

Now it's a game of cat and mouse, one where the cat cannot be caught. The consequences of being caught are too dire. No, this must be a killing that leaves absolutely no trace of me. At all.

He's back in that seat, the wingback chair I've seen him in several times before. The television flicks on. Porn. Young men displayed in disgusting positions on his television. Walking to his door, I test it and it's unlocked. Easy to get in. Easier than I anticipated. No force will be necessary... yet.

His walls are white. Sterile. Empty. No pictures are hanging. No love is felt in this house. It's cold. Barren. Depressing.

He has a child, why does it feel as if he has none.

The entrance to the main room where he's seated is wide open.

My hand grips the gun in hand, he hasn't noticed I'm there, standing at the main entrance watching him. He hasn't even felt my presence. With the flick of my wrist the light next to me flicks off and he moves turning fast in his chair. The asshole starts scrambling to his feet. He can't see me clearly, but he knows someone is there. Just has no idea who.

"You're in the wrong house, take what you want and leave."

I make no move to steal or leave. He's now standing, his face erratic, his eyes searching for something, possibly a weapon. It won't help. I'll kill him before he even touches it.

"Leave." Cunner's hand touches something next to him, the lights flick back on and now he can see me. He takes a step back, his head shaking back and forth. "I did nothing to that boy, didn't touch him." Those words leaving his mouth make my blood boil. I want to kill him again, and again, and once more for good measure. Even the thought of him going anywhere near my son makes me fill with rage. My cell starts ringing in my pocket, I know it's Rose without even looking at it. That doesn't mean I have to answer it. No. This time I won't be interrupted. This time I *will* finish what I started.

"The police will be here soon, I have alarms."

"It'll be quick."

"You don't have to do this. You don't have to go down this path. We all make mistakes." He thinks his words will persuade me otherwise. If I were a laughing man, I would do exactly that. Literally. But I'm not, so I give him no reply. My feet are heavy as I step closer to him. I want to look into his eyes as he takes his last breath, I want him to know that I'm the one stealing it from him. Then I want to watch as he's delivered to the same hell I will be visiting one day for all my misdeeds.

It takes a moment, and that moment is slow. My pulse quickens, but the world around me goes dead silent. It's a beautiful chaos. It's what I crave.

No one can take these moments from me, no matter how hard they try. It's next to impossible. The only thing that compares to this is *her*. Rose.

She's my favorite drug of choice. Even over this. Even over the silence of knowing I am playing God.

With one slip of my finger, I'm about to take away his life. And not once will I stop to think about why I did it. I will watch the life go from him. And I will walk out and have no problems sleeping at night.

Maybe I am the monster they tell me I am.

Maybe I can never change.

It won't stop me though, from what I'm about to do. What's about to happen.

The blood splatters behind him on the wall. It's a clean shot to the head. More than he deserves, but if he's right about the police, I need to move fast. Walking over to him, careful not to step in the blood that's now pooling at his head, I watch as his eyes, still open, lose the life that was left in them.

The color fades, no sign of life.

An adrenaline rush pulses through me. I did that. The power rush that comes with a kill. It's indescribable.

To some, it hurts their soul. Scars them. It's not something just anyone can do easily.

I was already fucked up, so doing this, doing what I do, my soul craves it. Which is the fucked up part of being who I am.

I leave the same way I came in, out the front door and intact. The asshole doctor, on the other hand, finally had his judgment day. And the mother that contracted me to kill him, well, she can keep her money.

Because this one, this one was way more personal in more ways than one.

12

ROSE

H is hands are all over me, my eyes are heavy as his kisses trail hot down my stomach. He left unexpectedly, deserting me to deal with the mother from hell. Sebastian seems like a sweet kid, not really sure where he got that from. They both eventually left not long after Liam did, leaving me pacing the room wondering where Liam went and why he wouldn't answer my phone calls. He only never answers when he's working, and Sax said he wasn't working.

Hot lips touch my nipple, his tongue circling it as he pushes himself on me. He's naked and hard right between my legs. He's stealing all my senses. I push him back, so his mouth isn't touching mine, and he looks down at me his eyes intense and heated.

"Where have you been?" I ask, the words falling from my lips.

Liam pushes down on me, making me groan at the feel of him between my legs. He reaches between us, pulling my shorts down my legs, then comes back. This time I can feel him, all of him. He's at my entrance, I open wider. Not meaning to, but with him, it's an automatic reaction. The smirk that touches his lips makes me know he knows he's just won.

How can I say no?

I can never say no.

In one swift movement, he's in me. Stealing me and not answering my question, distracting me from where he was and what he was doing.

"Rose." Opening my eyes, he's above me, his hands at my hips holding me to his own rhythm. I let him. It's what he needs, I can feel it.

Giving myself to him is something that comes naturally to me. I am his. It's imprinted on me from the very first moment I met him. Anyone before him was just a passing phase in my life directing me to where I was meant to be.

My hands grip his back as I lift to be closer to him, my nails digging into his flesh marking him as my own because that's what he is. Mine. He will always be mine. Even if I am going to have to pull the truth from him. I will.

My legs hold on tight, they grip around his waist as my hands drop to the sides and my orgasm hits me. Hard. He keeps going, taking the ride and making me come again as he does. His body lays heavily on mine, our breathing the same, erratic but sedated.

How can sex be this good?

With him, it's easy, natural. He owns me.

"Where have you been?" He makes no action to move. Stays exactly where he is, on me.

"Out."

Pushing him off me is harder than I thought. He doesn't make an attempt to move as I scoot backward under him. Sitting up and reaching for my robe, I wrap it around my waist. He watches me, not moving from the spot he's in.

"This is a first, I was wondering when you'd start hiding things from me."

His beautiful green eyes, the ones I love, the ones that can make me weak at the knees do nothing but stare at me. Liam isn't a man of words, but I like to think over the years he's changed some.

Maybe I was fooling myself.

Maybe I have my rose-colored glasses on and was blind to it.

"Rose."

My hand lies on the doorknob firmly. Letting it go, I turn back to him. I was ready to leave until he said my name.

"Don't go."

Liam Black isn't a man that tells you his needs. Ever. He doesn't show vulnerability. Liam Black is all man, one of the most frightening ones I've ever met. My love for him scares me the most. It frightens me so much I'm afraid I've put the blinders on myself.

"I don't think you should sleep in here, not if you can't tell me the truth."

He finally moves. Sitting up, he grabs a pair of boxers to put on. When he stands and walks over to me, my heart beats hard in my chest. His fingers drag down my cheek, then he lifts it up so I have to look at him.

"The less you know the better."

I shake my head. His finger doesn't drop from my chin as he holds on. Then he rubs my cheek with his fingers before he finally drops it. "Do I tell you how fucking beautiful you are?" A stray tear leaves my eye, but I don't even notice until he wipes it away and leans in to kiss where it was. "You are, so fucking beautiful. I wouldn't trade you for the world," he says, and my heart skips a beat. He still does that to me.

"But you hide things from me."

He doesn't falter as he nods his head. I guess in his way it's to protect me, but he shouldn't be doing that. We're a team now, have been for a long time. We walk through this life hand in hand, it's how we are.

"I'll tell you when I think it's time to tell you. Not a minute before, Rose." My eyebrow raises but he stays where he is right in front of me.

"Now we have that within our relationship, so if I choose not to tell you something that might affect you, you'll be fine with it?"

He nods his head. "If you thought it was best."

I laugh in his face.

Pulling the door open, I hold it for him. "Enjoy the couch."

"I love you, Rose."

I slam the door behind him, then regret it the moment I do. This Christmas is not going to be what I was hoping for.

My head hurts, my heart hurts. Damn.

13

BLACK

I f I told her and it led back to me, she could be in trouble. That's more than I'm willing to put her through. She isn't a risk I can take. Her life is top priority to me, always will be. The floor creaks behind me. Isabelle is there, I know it without even turning around. She's quiet, more so than the other two.

"You aren't sneaking out tonight." She turns on the lights, walking toward me. She's dressed but kicks off her shoes as she sits on one of the empty couches.

"You really made her angry. That's a first."

I nod, she's never kicked me out of our bed before. Threatened maybe. But then again, I haven't killed anyone behind her back for a long time. Especially when I said I would stop and didn't tell her.

"Are you ready for some serious ass kissing? You'll need it."

Shaking my head at her, I say, "Don't you have somewhere to be?"

She shrugs her shoulders. "Sebastian is too clingy, I need a break."

"You sound like the man in the relationship."

She giggles at my words. The bedroom door opens and Rose walks out. She's dressed, shoes on and ready to go.

I watch, waiting for her to look my way.

She has to look my way.

She doesn't.

Rose walks straight to the kitchen, pours herself a coffee and steps to the front door.

"Bye, Mom," Isabelle sings, looking at me.

"Bye, sweetheart, enjoy your day with your father." Then she walks outs and Isabelle laughs.

"Appears you're looking after us today. This should be fun."

I shake my head and go get dressed. When I'm done, all three of them are sitting at the counter waiting. For what? I'm not sure.

"Dad, breakfast. I'm starving."

"Do I look like your slave? You have two hands, right?"

Isabelle rolls her eyes. "Sunday is pancake day, with chocolate chip smiley faces. Mom usually does it. Guess it's your turn."

"Eat cereal or toast like normal people do."

Hayden looks up from his cell while little Liam scrunches up his nose in anger. Isabelle does nothing but smile.

"Fine." I proceed to cook the stupid pancakes, with stupid chocolate chip shit in them. Handing them over they all smile, then complain.

"Mom's smile is always happy, why does yours look so sad?" Little Liam complains by pushing the pancake back to me.

"Eat the pancake or starve."

His lip turns up and he doesn't budge from his decision.

"Right, starve it is."

"I'm telling Mom."

"Do it."

He pokes his tongue at me before he runs off back to his PlayStation.

"You know if he tells Mom you'll probably be in more trouble. You know... for starving your kids and all," Isabelle says, trying to contain her laughter.

"Liam, what do you want?"

He turns back to look at me. "A smiley face."

It takes two more times until I get the fucking smiley face to his approval. Then he only eats half of it anyway. Damn kid.

The rest of the day involves feeding Liam. How the hell he eats so much I have no idea. Where does he store it? He's almost like Jake in that way. Hayden goes to his girlfriend's to finish Christmas shopping. Isabelle sits on her cell complaining about Sebastian non-stop. Little Liam doesn't move from his game console.

It takes four more hours for Rose to walk back in that door. Not once has she rung or replied to my text messages. When she comes in, her hands are full of bags. Taking some of them for her, she looks at me then away.

"How was your day?"

Her words feel forced.

Placing it down, I step up behind her, my hands circling her waist and pulling her to me.

She breathes in heavily then expels a deep sigh. "It won't work this time." She makes no move to push me away, though.

"I love you, Rose."

She nods her head as I kiss her neck. Her ass pushes up against my cock.

"I know you do, Liam, as I love you. No one doubts that."

"Am I still banned from our bed?"

She nods. "Yes. Tell me where you were?"

I keep on kissing her, ignoring *that* question. She doesn't need to know.

"Okay, tell me this then... will you do it again?"

"I don't know what you're talking about."

She releases another deep sigh. "You'll be on the couch again. I hope you enjoyed it."

"It's Christmas tomorrow."

She shrugs her shoulders. "Tell me where you were, and we can make it the best Christmas ever."

Leaning back down, I kiss her neck but she pulls away. She never pushes away from my touch. Sometimes she tries to refrain from my touch, but that's only until we're in private. This is different.

"I take that back, despite you lying to me. It will be the best. I will make it the best. It has to be the best. We have Sandy coming tomorrow. I'm not sure how I feel about that. But she will *not* see cracks in our relationship."

Reaching for her hand, I spin her around so she has to look at me. She hasn't looked at me in the eye since she came back. Her vivid blue eyes stare up at me, lock me to her and hold me fucking tight.

"We don't have cracks, Rose. We don't crack."

She stares for a heartbeat before she finally nods her head. Then leans forward laying her head on my chest. "It's Christmas Eve, and I didn't even make the kids their pancakes."

"Let's not speak of pancakes for a long, long, time, please," I beg of her.

She leans back looking up to me, then laughs. There's a smile so big on her lips.

"Liam's very picky, you know this." She leans back on my chest. "You're still sleeping on the couch."

Kissing the top of her head, I try very hard to restrain from taking her right now, on this bench, in front of anyone that dares walk in the front door.

14

ROSE

I'm the first one up on Christmas Day every year, always have been. Sometimes Liam gets up to help me, sometimes he doesn't, it all depends on his work. When I walk out before the sun even hits the sky, dressed and ready to start setting up for the day, Liam's already up, the blankets on the couch folded up and the presents wrapped.

"You're up," I say looking at the Christmas tree. "And you helped... the presents," I say nodding to them.

"You've been stressed, I wanted to help."

I try to smile but it doesn't quite reach my eyes. "I have to start on the food. Kids will be up soon," I say walking away before I give in to him and not get the answers I'm wanting to hear. This time I want them–no, *need* them. Not giving in to him is hard, together we bounce from each other, level each other out.

He follows me in, he always does. His hands come to my face, his lips touch mine. Softly claiming me as his. It's not something he has to do, though. I'm already his, have been since we met. This setback won't ruin us, it's just a hurdle we need to get over. How long will it take us? I'm not sure. His kisses and touches are extremely difficult to say no to. My willpower isn't strong enough and he's fully aware of this fact. The kiss is light, he isn't demanding. He's claiming. I let him take from me what he obviously needs. Then when I know I will give him more, I pull back, breaking our kiss.

"Rose," he whispers reaching for me again.

"The bacon," I state with a smile and turn away to finish cooking.

He nods and walks off. I watch as he goes, admiring everything there is about him.

THE KIDS HAVE EATEN and opened their presents. Addy's over helping me set up for lunch while we wait for our guest. It feels weird, having someone else come into our house on this special day. We reserve it for those close to us, so Hayden letting Sandy come means he wants to get closer to her. It hurts, but I won't say no to him, I can't.

Addy is dressed in all white, while I have on a vibrant green dress and the kids are all wearing red. Liam, well, he's dressed in his usual attire—black like his namesake. That doesn't change. Some things will never change.

"Tell me, what's going on?" Addy asks.

I look past her to Liam. Hayden's sitting on the couch with Jake watching little Liam playing a game. They all laugh as Jake takes the remote.

"He's hiding something from me."

She stops what she's doing and looks up at me. Addy's mouth opens then closes.

"Say it, Addy."

"Well, Jake shook his head at an article in the paper the

other day and was muttering to himself. It could mean nothing, but when I saw it, it read 'Clean shot to the head. No evidence but investigating all leads.'"

"You think?"

She shrugs. "Maybe it's nothing. I only know what you guys say. What Jake and his club members say. Most are terrified of Black, you know that. So I'm not sure, but you shouldn't stress about it today, Rose. It's Christmas."

The doorbell rings, and Liam looks back to me knowing who it is. Hayden gets up, and I walk with him to the door as Addy finishes setting up for lunch. Hayden pulls it open to Sandy who's standing on the other side. A bottle of wine in her hand which she passes to Hayden.

"I wasn't sure what you wanted or needed."

"Thanks... S-Sandy." Hayden trips on his words, I can tell he's unsure of what to call her.

"Merry Christmas," I say leaning in and offering her a little side cuddle before I pull back letting her in. "I hope you're hungry, we've been cooking all morning."

Sandy nods her head with no true emotion in her eyes. She's thin, awfully thin, so much so she appears gaunt. When my arms wrapped around her, I could feel how emaciated she is. Her eyes are sunken, and it's obvious she hasn't had a proper meal for days. Her clothes are clean, but she smells of lingering cigarette smoke.

"Boys, Isabelle... why don't you all wash your hands and come to the table for lunch."

Hayden stays by my side as we stand awkwardly in the living room. Liam's the first person to come out. He walks straight to me, his hand coming to my waist as he leans down and kisses the top of my head.

"I never thought you'd settle down," Sandy speaks, looking around the house then coming back to us. Liam ignores her, smacking Hayden on the shoulder, then turns around and sits at the table.

Everyone comes out and the silence is almost awkward. We aren't used to having a guest on this day, but nevertheless, everyone starts grabbing food. Sandy's eyes keep looking up and finding Liam's who ignores her the best he can. And he's pretty good at ignoring people when he wants to.

"So what brings you back?" Jake asks Sandy while stuffing his face with a bread roll.

"Hayden, of course, and to see for myself that he survived."

Jake gives her a skeptical look. "Why wouldn't he survive?"

Sandy's eyes look to Liam then back to Jake. "I know who he is, don't think I don't."

"And you chose to leave your child with him?" asks Isabelle.

We all look her way, and she looks down to her food when Hayden taps her shoulder.

"He didn't give me much choice, did he?"

Jake laughs. "You took money over your child, sweetheart. Don't try to play coy with me." Everyone's silent as we listen. Hayden shifts in his seat, and I can feel he's getting uncomfortable.

"How about dessert?" I ask. No one answers as they all wait to see how she'll answer Jake.

"I knew who he was," is all she answers.

"Who was he then? You gave up your child," Hayden asks. He remembers how they were, how Sandy didn't care for him. He's hoping for a different outcome from her, I can tell.

She turns fast to Hayden's voice. "I'm here for you, to

make up for my mistakes."

"That wasn't the question," Hayden replies.

Sandy looks down at her food then back up. "You want answers? Is that why I'm here?"

Hayden nods his head. "You know I do, it's the reason you're here."

She starts shaking her head slowly. "I thought it would be a new beginning, a fresh start." Sandy looks over to Liam again, then around the table. "Maybe you don't want that, seeing as you have your fake family here. I'm your real family... I'm flesh and blood, after all."

Liam stands, pushes his chair back. His hands come down on the table as he leans over. "You are *not* his family. You are what made him. Nothing more. Don't dilute your recollections, Sandy. I fed him for years before I did anything about what you did to him. How you and whatever man you were fucking beat the crap out of him."

"I think you should leave," Hayden states. He looks down at Sandy as he stands. "I thought, maybe you wanted to try. But it's clear you came for something. What is it?"

Sandy places her hands on her lap as she fidgets with her shirt. "You don't get to ask me that," she says.

We all wait. Liam walks off not wanting to deal with her.

Hayden watches him go before he looks back to Sandy. "Why. Are. You. Here?"

"I need a little bit of money, just to get me by."

Hayden opens his wallet, throws whatever money he has in it at her then turns and walks away.

Her voice stops him. "I need more than that."

He halts.

Hayden reminds me of Liam when he turns around and gives her a vacant stare. "Get out and don't come back."

I hear a knock on the door, Addy's the first to move to answer it.

Sandy stands collecting the money from the table and the floor then looks at us watching her. "I never wanted a kid, he was never meant to be born."

My heart hurts at hearing those words, I'm just thankful he isn't here to hear them.

"You need to leave, Sandy, and you better never come back. No more money will be handed to you."

"The next time I see you, I won't be so polite," Jake says smiling.

Hayden's girlfriend walks in, looks around and walks away to Hayden's room.

"Oh, you won't be hearing from me again. That you *can* count on."

"Good, besides my daddy will kill you," says Isabelle as she smiles, picking up a piece of turkey.

Sandy runs off not even shutting the door behind her.

My heart's been hurting a lot lately, I don't think I can keep Liam out tonight.

I need him.

15

BLACK

Pacing back and forth is all I can do right now, it's fucking Christmas. Today is not the day to go and kill some fucker. Especially a woman that needs not one but many bullets to her stinking skull. A soft knock comes on the door then it's pushed open, and Rose comes in, shutting the door behind her.

"You did really well." Her words help the anger that's built and ready to explode. "She's gone, but you were right, she came for money. You might want to check on Hayden."

Of course, she did, it's the only reason she would want to come back. That woman doesn't have a bone in her body that's motherly, she should have had her vagina cut from her fucking body to stop her from having kids.

Rose rises up, kisses my lips then holds the door open for me, basically telling me to go to Hayden.

Walking to his room the door is closed. So I knock on it. Miranda answers and looks straight to the floor. She pulls the door open fully then steps around it.

Hayden looks up from his bed where his head is in his hands. "You were right. Happy?"

Stepping into his room, I shut the door behind me. Then sit on his office chair opposite him. "I take no fucking pleasure in knowing that." He looks down, then back up to me. Torment is clear, pain is evident in his eyes. "What does it matter, Hayden? What does it fucking matter what she wanted? You don't need her."

He shakes his head. "You don't get it, you don't fucking get it. You may have taken me from that life, but I am hers, Black. She created me, and I hoped at one stage she may have even loved me."

My fists slam down hard on his desk, I feel the crack of wood beneath them. "We love you, your fucking mother loves you. Not her. You know this."

A stray tear leaves his eye. "You don't love us, you love killing. Does Mom know you've been doing it again? Have you told her?"

A gasp is heard when the door is pushed open as Rose steps in.

"I was coming to make sure everything was okay and I overheard." Her eyes find mine. "Is that true, Liam? Are you killing again?"

I stand from the desk and look back to Hayden. "I'm not Black to you. I am your fucking guardian. Do you hear me?"

"I'm sorry, Dad. I just—"

"I know, just don't fucking go there again. Now take the kids to Jake's while I speak to your mother."

Hayden gets up to leave, and Rose crosses her hands over her chest as she waits for the front door to shut.

"So you're back? Back to being the old you. Should we go back to separate lives again? Maybe that's what you want?"

I shake my head.

How can she see it that way?

Then she gasps. "You killed him, didn't you? That man

that drugged Hayden. You killed him?" I nod my head. "How could you, I asked you not to."

"He didn't deserve to live."

"You don't get to decide that, Liam. You are *not* God. You are *not* who you used to be. You stopped. Why did you go back?"

The truth spills from my lips before I have a chance to stop it. "I missed it. I fucking missed it."

"I hope it was worth it. I hope you will take great pleasure that you have single-handedly ruined Christmas for me. Now get the fuck out of my house, because you're not the man I knew. You are selfish."

"Rose."

She shakes her head. "I'm afraid right now I will say something I can't take back. So it's best you leave right *now* before I do."

My feet start moving even if I don't want them to. Leaving her on Christmas day is the last thing I want to do.

It's getting dark as I exit the house, the kids are playing in Jake's front yard when I walk over. Addy turns and smiles before she calls the kids to her. Walking inside, Jake's ready with a bottle of beer in hand.

"Addy will go and spend the night with her, don't even stress." He knows before I even ask.

"Maybe I should marry you."

He spits out his drink. "You were going to ask her to marry you?"

I pull out the ring from my pocket. It's been burning a hole in there for days.

Tonight was going to be the night.

Now it's not.

It's ruined.

"Holy fuck. Holy fuck." He shakes his head. "You sure as hell fucked up killing those assholes then." I don't even bother to deny it in front of him, he knows me better than that.

"What am I meant to do?"

Jake starts laughing. "You're asking me for advice? You must be desperate."

I punch him on the arm as Hayden walks in. Jake looks back to his television as Hayden waits for me to speak.

Hayden fucked up, badly.

But he was hurting.

His hopes were up, and then they were crushed right in front of him.

Hope is not something I like, it ruins people's lives. Maybe that's where I went wrong. I hoped that the day would go smoothly, and of course, it did anything but do that.

"You're mad." His eyes find the ring that's still in my hand. "Fuck, were you going to—"

"He sure fucking was. About time too if you ask me," Jake pipes in.

I restrain myself from hitting him again.

"Did I fuck this up?" The pain in Hayden's voice is evident, it hurts him more than his rent-a-womb mother.

"No, you didn't. I did."

Hayden's eyes lift from the ring in my hand. "She's going to be so upset. We ruined Christmas. It's her favorite day of the year."

We all go silent.

It is.

And we've royally fucked it up for her.

"You better fix it. And it's best to start on her favorite day, so it's not ruined forever," Jake says as Hayden sits next to me.

I tap his leg letting him know he's okay and he offers me a restrained smile.

16

ROSE

I f I could pull my hair out I would. I pick up the wine bottle and drink it straight from the bottle. Addy walks in after playing with the kids and putting little Liam in his room, with a bottle of wine in her hand. She laughs when she sees me. "I see you've got a head start on me already."

I hold up the almost empty bottle. "Time for you to catch up." So she does just that and soon we're both drunk, so fucking drunk that when Liam walks in, I don't kick him out. Addy merely gets up and leaves or stumbles—not sure which really.

"Rose."

Rolling my eyes at him, "Rose. Rose. Rose. That word dripping from your lips doesn't make everything okay, Blac—"

"How much have you had to drink?"

I grab the Christmas ham and start eating it. "What a waste."

He picks up some of it and starts eating as I swat his hand away. "Go away, Liam Black."

"No, Rose, I will not."

I poke my tongue out at him and he gets up, walking around to me. "Don't touch me." I know I'm being childish, but I just can't help it.

"I want to touch you." His hands do exactly what he says. He touches. And despite myself, I don't knock him away. He spins me around so we're face to face. "I will touch you because I fucking love you."

"You love yourself more," I say against his lips.

"That's not humanly possible." He picks me up, starts carrying me to our room. He lays me on the bed and begins undressing me until I'm naked.

"Do you plan on fucking me now? Hard. Pull my hair maybe?" I get up on all fours, crawling to him. "Maybe spank my ass while you're at it?"

Liam growls when I turn, pushing my ass at him. "You, my love, are going to bed. Tomorrow if you are up to it, I'll spank your ass and pull your hair all you fucking want."

"Promises, promises," I mutter, dropping on my stomach and closing my eyes.

Liam pulls the blanket up over me, and that's all I remember.

"Mom, Mom, Dad's doing Christmas again. Get up. Get up." Groaning as I move, next to me is something for my headache, plus a glass of water. Little Liam leaps on my bed and starts jumping with excitement.

"What are you talking about, baby?" Reaching for my clothes, I pull them on while little Liam doesn't stop bouncing around with enthusiasm.

"Dad set it all up. You slept so long, Mom. It's lunchtime

already. Dad said we can't eat until you get up. So, get up, Mom." Then he's gone, running out the door.

Going to the bathroom, I quickly wash my face before I walk back out.

Little Liam was right, everyone's here.

My eyes find *him*, he's in the kitchen watching me already.

"What's going on?"

"We're doing Christmas today."

"It's not Christmas," I say walking over.

Jake and Addy smile as they sit at the table with the kids. Even Meredith is there.

"Redo," Liam says like it's as simple as that.

"You can't redo Christmas," I say shaking my head.

"We can and we will," he retorts back to me.

"Fine, let's have a new Christmas."

If Liam smiled, he would smile now. We all sit down and eat and it's better. Way better. Jokes are told and everyone's laughing.

"Mom, can we do this every year?" Little Liam asks before he kisses my cheek and runs off. Everyone else has gone silent, the tension seems thick.

"Isabelle, Hayden... can you please leave and give us a few minutes?"

Isabelle stands walking off. Hayden is hesitant, though.

"We just need to talk, just the parents."

Hayden stands, looks to Jake and smiles. "He shouldn't be here then."

Jake flips him off making us smile before he walks out.

"How many? I need to know how many."

Addy looks down, Jake doesn't say a word, just watches. He knows better than to talk. Liam, on the other hand, his eyes don't leave mine, he knows not to lie to me. The truth is what I want, and if it's what I don't get I'm afraid of where that will leave us.

"Is this something you really need to know, Rose?" he asks as if he believes his words are true. That it's something I don't need to know.

Looking away, the house is the same, the decorations still on the walls and food everywhere. It looks like Christmas, even tastes like Christmas. But is it really? No. It's not. That day was ruined, and my son was hurt in the process.

"Tell me. And do it fast like you're ripping off a Band-Aid."

He sucks in a breath, and I know whatever's about to leave his mouth I won't like. Not at all. "I've killed three people. Each one worse than the last."

"Th-Three," I say after him, my voice breaks in disbelief. Shaking my head, I stand. My legs push the chair back and it falls over. My legs are shaky, but I manage to stay standing. "You killed... three people?"

He nods his head. "You knew who I was to begin with. I tried to stop. I did stop for ages. It just... crept back in."

My head starts shaking back and forth. "Do you want that life? You don't want this life with us anymore?" I try my hardest not to let the tears fall, to keep them inside but Liam notices and he stands and walks over to me. He looks down at Jake and Addy, nods his head to the door and within seconds they're gone, leaving us alone.

"Never say that, you are my life. That, I just can't help."

"I'm trying to understand, really I am. But you chose this, you chose us over that. It sounds to me like you want to go back to that other life." I search his eyes for some truth like I can see what he's thinking. I can't. "It's okay if you do, Liam. It's what you know. I've been proud of the person you are, always have been. But if you choose to do that again, I can't have you living here. I can't have that in my life and our children's lives."

This time his hands drop from holding my arms.

He steps back.

"You…" is all he says.

My ears ring from my heart beating too hard in my chest. It's almost deafening.

"Me," I say in a small voice. Taking a step back from him.

As I look down at the floor, hands wrap around my waist and cup my ass, he lifts me up as I wrap my legs around his waist.

"You, Rose. I pick you. It was an itch I had to scratch. It's scratched. It was the last time. I promise with your heart, and you know I'd never want to hurt that." His hand comes up and wipes a tear that went rogue down my cheek. "Don't cry for me, those tears are wasted."

I shake my head. "Nothing is wasted on you, Liam. You're worth every tear and then some."

His lips touch mine, and I take all that he's willing to give.

17

BLACK

Have you ever seen an angel? Felt one? Been consumed by one? I have and as of this very moment I'm being consumed on a daily basis. Whenever she touches, kisses, or even looks at me. It's what she does, she devours me.

Her hands grip my back as I slide into her, nails digging in leaving her imprint. She hasn't fully forgiven me, I can feel the tension still in her. But she's willing to try.

I don't deserve her.

I never have and never will.

Trying to be the better man for her is all I can be.

It's what she needs.

Sliding in and out of her I can feel her tighten around me, she's close. Her hair is fanned all around her, her eyes closed while riding the wave. Then it hits her. Her pussy squeezes me tight. Fucking ecstasy.

"Black," she says as she comes. I don't think she even realizes she says that name, she never calls me that. It's always Liam.

Biting her nipple, she arches as I come inside her,

clinging to me as I take what's left. Everything that's possible.

Turning over, I lay her on my chest. Her finger draws lines around my nipple.

"It never gets old. You know. Us. Never."

I nod my head. "I don't think it ever will. I can't imagine a time I wouldn't want you."

"I'm still mad. Don't think I'm not." She looks up at me then turns around and lays back on me.

"Forgive me. You being mad is not something I want."

"It's not as easy as that."

Sitting up, I take her with me as she wraps herself around me. "Tell me what I can do... to make you forgive me."

"It hurt. You hurt me. I didn't realize you'd hide things from me, then lie to me on top of that." Brushing her hair away with my fingers, I kiss the tip of her nose.

"There's no excuse for doing what I did, but I felt like I had to do it. I didn't tell you because I knew it could put you in a position you didn't need to be in."

She looks at me unblinking. "Next time, tell me how you feel, instead of going off and doing something like that again. Okay?" she asks.

"Yes. I will come to you when I feel the urge to kill." I tell her the truth. She visibly relaxes then slides forward over my hardening cock.

"I'm sure I can always make you feel better, in more ways than one." And she does, with her mouth, her hands, and her sweet, sweet pussy.

"IT HAS TO BE PERFECT, everything has to be perfect."

"Fuck! You sound like a bitch," Jake mutters while cleaning the backyard. Addy helps me decorate, adding roses and fairy lights everywhere. Rose is out with Casey right now, and not due back until after dinner. The kids, Addy and Jake have been over here helping me set the backyard up for the last hour, and for the last hour Jake has bitched and moaned the whole time.

"If I had a gun," I mutter to him.

He rolls his eyes. "Yeah, yeah... if you had a gun. Well, listen up. I have my fists, want me to use them?" Jake starts bouncing back and forth from foot to foot like he's a pro fighter.

"What on earth are you doing, looks like you're trying to get away from a bee," Addy says holding the roses in her hand.

"Woman." He stops bouncing and looks down at her with a warning glare.

"Did I tell you about that, Black? How Jake here jumps and screams like a little girl when there's a bee around?"

"Woman, I'm about to take you home and spank your fucking ass. Stop ruining my street cred."

Hayden laughs, and Jake turns giving him a death stare.

"Did I tell you about that time with the banana—" Before she can finish, Jake's picked her up and thrown her over his shoulder.

"We'll be back. Give me an hour. Need to spank some sense into this woman."

"Only an hour," Addy says with a giggle and waving to us as they go. We hear the spank of her ass and the small chuckle that follows as they walk off toward their house.

"I want to love someone the way you both do," Hayden says. Watching the space where Jake disappeared into.

"Oh, you will. If someone like me can find someone as

fucking fabulous as your mother, I have no doubt you will, too. And maybe you won't fuck it up like I did."

"Maybe." He shrugs his shoulders.

"Meredith, isn't it? Is she?"

He looks up to me and doesn't bother lying. "I want her to be. I try to love her the same way she does me. I just don't think it's going to happen. She's not it."

"I can't say I know what that feels like. I've never tried to love anyone. Rose was the only woman I ever thought of. She was it from the moment I saw her sitting in the fucking rain."

"I remember how you were, before her. I was young, but I remember."

Looking up at him, I didn't think he would remember. Bits and pieces maybe.

"You were the scariest person I'd ever seen, but you were also the safest person I could be with. I knew that, even then."

I grab his neck and pull him to me in a hug. He's shocked at first, locking his body as if he's ready for a fight. Then he relaxes and wraps his arms around me tightly.

"I don't know where I'd be without you. I don't even want to wonder. Most likely dead. I owe you everything, Black."

"You owe me nothing, except maybe helping me finish this fucking yard." Pushing him away he nods his head.

"She's going to flip. You don't ever do this shit for her."

"Does that make me... bad?" I ask, wondering. I didn't know this was something people did.

Hayden laughs. "No, you don't need to do it. That's a plus with loving someone the same way they love you, I guess."

Maybe he's right, I never thought she needed anything... romantic. But I could have been wrong all this time.

18

ROSE

"You've forgiven him already?" Casey asks as she drives me home after a few wines. She was away for Christmas and got back today—we always spend Boxing Day together. Until, well, we decided to have a new Christmas Day because the first one was ruined.

"Not so much forgiven, more like accepted. I knew who he was. He's been so good. He slipped. I don't think he'll do it again."

Casey raises an eyebrow as we pull up to my driveway. "You chose to be with a man who was known for exactly what you wanted him to stop being?"

"Exactly. So that's why I can't be too mad. Yes, I am mad that he did it, but I can't leave him over it."

"Plus, there's that big fat factor..." she wiggles her eyebrows at me, "... that you love the shit out of him."

Leaning over I kiss her cheek before I get out. "That's a major factor. Actually, the only factor, to be exact." Getting out and shutting the door, I look back through the window. "And I love you, too. Thank you." I wait until she's gone before I walk into the house. It's dark when I enter. Looking down at the floor, I notice there are tea light candles making a pathway. My heart jumps from my chest, I have to catch it and bring it back as I follow the lights to the backyard. The first person I see is Hayden. He smiles. My fingers brush his hand as I keep walking. Isabelle is next, then little Liam. Looking past him as I clutch his little hand in mine. I notice rose petals cover the ground, so I follow them with my eyes until I see *him*.

Liam's standing at the end, the gorgeous little lights stop at him. It's ironic really because all my light does stop with him.

"What's going on?" I ask as I continue to walk to him.

He grips my hand in his, his smile is easy when it touches his lips. "I don't know why I haven't done this sooner. Forgive me?"

"Be romantic? I don't need romance from you, Liam."

"Don't expect it often." He winks at me. It makes me giggle because it's true.

This is extremely unexpected.

But what comes next is totally unanticipated.

His hand touches my face, his fingers linger on my lip before he drops down on one knee.

My hands fly to my mouth, a gasp so loud follows. Then he opens a box, a box with the most stunning ring I've ever seen. It's shaped like a snowflake. There's a diamond in the center with black diamonds surrounding it. Its dazzling brilliance is almost blinding as it twinkles and sparkles in the light.

"Rose, our love is one for the books. No one can love someone the way I love you. It's not humanly possible. I tried to stop myself from loving you all those years ago, that was a mistake. You see, you're etched so fucking far in here..." he points to his heart, "... that there's no way you're getting out. And I don't want you out. But I also want to promise you, that those things I've done, I won't do again. Because knowing I'm the one that hurt you, hurts more than you can ever possibly imagine. I just want to know one thing, Rose..." He pauses, and I nod my head for him to continue.

My heart's in my hands as I watch him, he looks so flawless. His black suit clinging to him in all the perfect ways, and here he is bending on one knee on the ground in front of me. Like I'm the only person to bring him to his knees.

"Will you marry me?"

My eyes leave him, the kids now standing close. Waiting and watching for my answer, while I try to blink away the tears that pool in my eyes as I lean down. Gripping his face with my fingers, I start talking, "I will, Liam Black. Because I love you. Today. Tomorrow. The next day. And every day after that."

The kids start clapping and whistling. His arms circle around me as he picks me up and spins me around. Then he stops and kisses me. He tastes like my tears and everything that's the sweet Liam Black. Gripping his face, I show him how much I love him with just our lips.

Not once did I think he would propose to me.

Ever.

The dream of a wedding, well, I never really had that.

Not that I didn't see a future with him, just that I was happy being us. Knowing that was enough for me, no ring or a certificate could change that fact, at all.

"Can you believe Dad did that? This is the best Christmas ever," Isabelle says, smiling. She turns and walks inside with the other two, leaving us standing in the yard by ourselves with me still wrapped around him.

"You did all this? You know I didn't need it, right?"

He grips my ass, pinching it. "I know you didn't need it, or maybe even want it. But I need and want you to be officially mine... in every way humanly possible. So if you ever leave, I'll find you."

I laugh at his words. "As if I would ever leave you." I kiss his nose then kiss my way back to his lips.

"I would find you. It's what I'm good at," he says between kisses.

"I would hope you'd find me because I'm always going to be yours."

19

ROSE

ne year later...

WE MADE Christmas even more special this year. My green dress scrapes the floor as I fix Isabelle's lipstick. She's dressed in the perfect shade of red which blends in well with her hair and her blue eyes. I see beauty in all that she is.

"Wow, Mom," little Liam says from behind me. He runs to me hugging me tightly.

"You'll wrinkle her dress."

I shake my head at Isabelle's words.

"Dad's waiting. It's time," Hayden says, opening the door. Little Liam and Isabelle walk out, leaving Hayden and me standing here.

"You look beautiful, Mom, truly beautiful."

I kiss his cheek as he places his hand in mine. We step out of the tent I used to get dressed in. A red carpet is laid perfectly on the ground ready for me to walk on. Scattered on the carpet are rose petals shaped in small love hearts, and there are arches with flowers dangling all over them along the way. Honestly, it's stunning.

Looking up the hill, the same hill we've been to several times before, the one that if you jump, you'll end up in a bottomless waterhole. It's the same one we swam in as kids then as adults. It's where we chose to be married. It has both good and bad memories attached to it. But it's ours.

All our friends wait for me as Hayden walks me to *him*, my green dress clings to my body showing my bare back. The lace trails down my arms to my wrists. The fabric of the dress lengthens to the floor, and a small train drags behind me. It's not your typical white dress. No. It's what we like. We aren't normal, so why would we make this anything like normal.

Liam smiles the minute his eyes touch mine, then the most marvelous thing happens, a tear leaves his eye, one so small that if you weren't watching you'd surely miss it. Hayden stops me from going straight into his arms and holds me to him. He kisses my cheek then releases me to Liam. Who I go to gladly.

"You look beautiful."

I assess him in his black suit. "You don't look so bad yourself."

"We tried to get him to wear pink," Jake says from behind us.

Everyone laughs as Liam cringes.

"No more pink for you, okay, babe?"

He nods his head and everything else goes silent. Nothing else exists as the ceremony goes on. And soon after, before we have to meet everyone at the reception, we wait for everyone to depart, leaving just us remaining. He undoes the back of my dress as the sun starts to set. It floats to the ground at my feet while he undresses. I purposely wore nothing underneath, and when he pushes against me I can feel his excitement. He pushes me forward until my feet hit the edge of the cliff. Looking down, the green water almost looks black as the sun sets.

Liam's hand wraps in mine as he steps in next to me. "One last time."

"One last time." I nod then we jump, together holding hands until I can no longer see anything but the blackness. Coming up for air, he isn't up, but I don't panic. He'll come up when he's ready. The blackness calls to him more so than anyone else.

His dark hair is the first thing that surfaces, and as he does, he pulls me to him. Our bodies connecting, joining as one.

"Liam," I say as I feel him, right in that spot.

"Wife," he says as he enters me. That word leaving his lips is something I never thought I would hear. It's not something I craved for. Ever. But it was something I sometimes thought about.

He makes love to me, with a need and domination I've never felt before. He does more than consume me, he owns me. Whole.

My hands find the rock behind me and I cling to it as I let him have me. When we come, he bites my shoulder, hard. Then he licks that exact same spot, soothing it with his mouth.

"We have a wedding reception to get to," I say as he holds me while we float on the water just being with one another in the calmness of night. I'm glad I didn't wear much make-up, it would have been a waste.

"Why, I own you now."

I giggle at his words. "You already did. Now you have a piece of paper to prove it," I say climbing up on the rocks. He smacks my ass and follows me up. Liam helps me into my dress, zipping it up before he gets dressed.

Our car is in the same spot it was when we arrived.

"Are you ready for a whole new chapter of our lives, Mrs. Black?" he asks me.

My hair is soaking wet and dripping down my back. I wipe it away as I answer him, "I've always been ready, Mr. Black. Now, why don't we go celebrate with those we love."

"Those we love. Who would have thought I was capable of loving more than you?"

I wink as I grab his hands. "I always knew you could. You just took some time to see it for yourself."

***

THE END.

ALSO BY T.L SMITH

Other books by TL Smith

Sasha's Dilemma (Dilemma #1)

Adam's Heaven (Dilemma #1.5)

Sasha's Demons (Dilemma #2)

Kandiland

Pure Punishment (Standalone)

Antagonize Me (Standalone)

Degrade (Flawed #1)

Twisted (Flawed #2)

Black (Black #1)

Red (Black #2)

White (Black #3)

Distrust (Smirnov Bratva #1)

Disbelief (Smirnov Bratva #2)

Defiance (Smirnov Bratva #3)

Dismissed (Smirnov Bratva #4)

Lovesick (Standalone)

Lotus (Standalone)

Savage Collision (A Savage Love Duet book 1)

Savage Reckoning (A Savage Love Duet book 2)

Buried in Lies

Distorted Love (Dark Intentions Duet 1)

Sinister Love (Dark Intentions Duet 2)

Connect with T.L Smith by tlsmithauthor.com

ACKNOWLEDGMENTS

There are so many I want to thank while on this journey, especially those who took a chance on Black. He was so unknown when I wrote him, but he bled onto my pages like he was always meant to be there. I just didn't know until quite some time after. So, out of thanks, I wanted to write this short story for those who love him as much as I do, and as a thank you for all your support since Black. He truly is a man I loved writing. And I hope you love him as much as I do. So thank you to you, for reading. To sticking with me through it all. It's because of you reading this right now that I continue to write men who aren't perfect and woman who are strong. (Woman power!)

Lots of love,
    T.L Smith x

DISTORTED LOVE EXCERPT

AVAILABLE NOW.

Prologue

Saskia

My hands run the length of the cold cement wall at the back of the alley. I'm in a place I don't recognize but I was requested to meet here. Straightening my posture, I brush my fingers through my blonde hair and take another step, one foot in front of the other in my high heels. These things cost me more than a pretty penny with their signature red soles. So here I am because I received an email telling me the location.

It has to be her.

Or so I thought.

It's been one year since I've seen her. Or him for that matter. They ran off together. I loved him as much as I loved her. It wasn't fair. They broke my heart.

Checking my phone, I pause with one hand on the cement wall and notice I have no reception. Great. Just what I need. Rummaging through my bag, I check for my wallet, and find my pills and bottle of water as well. Hey, at least I have water. If I die today, I'll be hydrated.

It's late. My last client was finalized before I left to come here. So, after this, I plan to go and sit in my bath and drink all the fucking wine.

If I make it out alive, that is. Looking up, there's a white door a short distance away from me. It has a sign hanging from a rusty nail that states 'Knock Three Times.' I want to laugh and purposely knock only once, or twice, to be a smart ass. I restrain myself. Instead, I go against my better judgment and knock three times like the sign says.

Standing there, I wait for the door to magically open. It doesn't. Instead, nothing happens. So I knock again. This time, four times for good measure. I chuckle. Nothing.

Turning around, I notice the door I entered through is now shut.

Fuck! I swear I left it open. How did that happen?

A scream rips from my mouth.

Quinn is standing in front of me.

That same deadly stare he had all those years ago still in place.

He's dangerous.

He's a collector. And not of things. Of people.

"Saskia." He says my name then steps back, pushing the door open to a dark room.

I don't want to walk in there. Who the fuck knows what's in that room, and I sure as shit don't want to find out. I'm more than happy keeping all my body parts today, thank you very much.

Turning, a voice stops me.

It isn't Quinn's.

No, it's *him*.

Emotions slam into me.

Hate.

Love.

Lust.

Anger.

He holds them all. He's the reason I'm the person I am today.

"*Barbie...*" A shiver runs over my skin, and the hairs on the back of my neck stand up like little soldiers.

Ryken Lord is back.

But what for?

"Ryken," I say, spinning around and staring into the darkened room. He lights a small candle, the flicker letting me make out his shape as I step into the room. Quinn shuts the door behind me and effectively locks us in.

"You shouldn't have come back." He steps forward, and my heart slams into my chest.

Boom.

Boom.

Boom.

Three pumps, one for each time he broke the fucking thing.

His lip twitches. My heart stutters. Our eyes meet.

Ridiculous manic girl meets stupid criminal boy.

"How could I stay away, *Barbie*? Surely you knew I'd be back, for you."

I shake my head at his words. "Where is she?"

He shakes his head. "I'm here to discuss us."

My head shakes slowly, and I step back to the door, reaching out for the handle. I pull it open, looking back to the man that I want to stab in the eye, but fuck at the same time.

"You sir, can go fuck yourself in the ass. Don't fucking contact me again!"

Quinn smirks as I walk past him.

"You owe me, *Barbie*."

Turning back, I see him standing at the door, and it's now I notice that he's dressed in all black. The way he should be. He smirks knowing he has me now.

"And I've come to collect what's mine."

Shaking my head, I run. Away from him, and away from my shattered heart that I

left with him.

Because Ryken is not a man to be trusted. He's proven that on many occasions.

Every time he's managed to break my heart.

Then he gave his to *her*.

Chapter 1

Ryken

Bending her over, legs spread, my hand on her ass, that's how I've imagined her. Her perfect round ass up in the air for my viewing pleasure.

Saskia Tyler—a *Barbie* bombshell.

The boys know her as Tyler, I know her as *Barbie*.

She bends down to pick up something, and my head goes crazy with thoughts. Of how her tight little tits will fit perfectly in my hand, to how her pink nipples will feel with my mouth wrapped around them. The things I can do to her. The things my hands, mouth, and tongue can do to her. They could punish her, the way she likes it.

I hate her just as much as I want to fuck her.

She's off limits, yet ever so enticing.

No words have ever passed between us. No glances from her direction. She doesn't see anyone but herself. Or should I say, she doesn't want to be seen by anyone else.

But I've seen her, with her long blonde hair and the way she always straightens her clothes. I imagine those hands running all over me the same way she has them running all over *her*.

My nails pick at the orange in my hand while I watch her walk in the rain, her hair becoming wet, but she doesn't care like other girls do. No, she just runs a hand over her head then continues on like she's not sopping wet and walks into school.

Stalker, that's what I've become.

How did that ever happen without me realizing?

Seeing her one day and stalking her the next.

The first time I saw her she was standing behind Livia Tyler, her cousin. She was looking down at the floor, and I immediately thought how submissive she'd be in the bedroom. How I could bend her over and take her from behind, without so much as a struggle. She would take it, and she would love it. She just doesn't know it yet.

Livia, on the other hand, I'm not sure... would be work? Not that I don't like some work to get who I want. I just prefer my women one way.

Girls have never been a problem, to try or to taste. Not once have I had an issue bedding a woman. They have always come willingly, from the moment I started to realize what my cock was for, and, man, have I used it.

I excel at sex.

But her...

I would love it so much more if Saskia Tyler were in my bed.

I love to hate her.

There's nothing in between.

My hand itches to touch myself, to wrap my hands around my cock and stroke it right here and now as I watch Saskia walk the halls of school with her head down watching each step she takes.

Does she know I hate her, but at the same time want her?

I have to adjust myself because she's getting closer, and if she looks up and notices me the way I am right now—she may very well hate me as much as I hate her.

Saskia aka *Barbie* Tyler.

I want to bend and snap her in ways that shouldn't be legal or even written about. I want to fuck her so hard, all she can see and hear is me. Nothing else should leave those lips all night. Nothing but *my* name.

Saskia turns to look behind her, her hair falls in front of her face, and she pulls it back so it doesn't go in her eyes.

I want to pull at it.

Hard and unwavering.

Shaking my head, I stand back. There are other students walking in behind her. Her cousin isn't too far back and her friend, the gay one, is talking to someone else. She hasn't noticed them yet, but she will.

Could I steal a few moments with her, just to smell the vanilla that lingers on her skin? The things I could do if I only had one taste.

"Ryken." I hear my name called and it's one of the teachers. My cock's hard as granite, so I try to think about dead cats to see if it will soften. It doesn't work because I'm about to lose my opportunity to speak to Saskia. To touch her, to make sure she's real and not some made-up perfect doll I've created in my head.

My very own sex toy *Barbie* doll.

Mmm, doesn't that sound enticing?

Nodding my head to the teacher once, I step out of the room looking straight at Saskia. She's walking my way, her head down. Her hands on her clothes trying to get rid of the water that's not moving. It will dry eventually, but she wants it gone straight away.

Looking past Saskia, her cousin glances up and I watch the way she stares at me. It's the same way my father's female employees look at me. They want something, or me. Looking back down, I step over to her. If she looks up right at this second, she'll see that I've done it on purpose, and that I could have stopped if I chose to. I just decided not to. My body wants to slam into hers to feel every curve she has to offer, instead of hiding behind her frumpy uniform.

She almost stumbles but manages to right herself.

I ran into her on purpose.

I touched her on purpose.

Every action has a reaction.

As she looks up at me with those mocha-colored eyes, I know right here, and now, even if I tried to convince myself I hate her, I would never be able to achieve it.

Made in United States
Orlando, FL
09 December 2022

25849408R00061